Filthy Money

Lissa Brown

Quest Books
by Regal Crest

ISBN 978-1-61929-446-2

First Edition 2020

9 8 7 6 5 4 3 2 1

Cover design by AcornGraphics

Published by:

Regal Crest Enterprises

Find us on the World Wide Web at
http://www.regalcrest.biz

Published in the United States of America

Acknowledgments

Writing is often described as a solitary pursuit, but I've never written a book without lots of help and support from friends, family and sometimes complete strangers.

Bette Jo Bachman of Monroe County, Pennsylvania provided research assistance that saved me an additional trip to Stroudsburg, PA. Other research support came from Maria DeBella, Joe Scaccia, John Morrone, Chuck Lowenstein, Shelley Scalera and Barry Brown. Karen Hoose, pastoral associate at the Church of the Holy Spirit in Gloversville, New York provided important information about cemeteries there. I'm grateful to the focus group of Italian-American friends who helped me with language and customs and tried to steer me away from potentially offensive stereotypes. If I strayed, it's not their fault. Thanks to K. G. MacGregor for her encouragement.

My deepest appreciation goes to members of critique groups and other beta readers for their invaluable input. They've helped me through the writing of this story from first drafts through countless revisions to the completed manuscript. Ingrid, Ree, Terri, Diane, Sharon and Carole, you're the best. In addition, members of the High Country Writers in North Carolina provided guidance and support. My wonderful writing partner lent me the benefit of her critical eyes and encouraged me to stretch. Thanks, SLH.

I thank my neighbors who did their best to keep their dogs quiet while I labored during warmer months with all windows open.

My spouse, Mary Ann, stayed quiet and did my share of so many chores while I was immersed in pursuit of the world's greatest novel. She proofread the final manuscript through her eyes as a former English teacher. She cheered me when I was frustrated and embraced me with love as she has for thirty-five years.

Chapter One

Newark, New Jersey - 1953

"CLOSE THE DOOR," Trish shouted and pushed past Gabby as she rushed into their apartment dragging a heavy black duffle bag.

Gabby engaged the deadbolt and both chain locks. "What's going on? Everything go okay with the funeral home guys?"

"Yeah, fine. I even learned that Salvatore Centimiglia wasn't Mr. C's real name. It was Nicolo Catania."

"How come he changed it?"

Trish shrugged. She retrieved a crumpled note from her pocket and handed it to Gabby. Gabby set it on the dinette table and smoothed it out so she could read it. "Is this serious?" she asked, her eyes widening way beyond their normal size.

"Serious as a heart attack." Trish unzipped the bag and reached in to pull out a handful of bills, all fifties and hundreds. She wrinkled her nose and tried to fan away the musty smell that wafted out of the bag.

"Is this real money?" Gabby gasped and took a few of the bills from Trish.

"It's not Monopoly money." Trish reached into the bag and pulled out more of the smelly bills.

"Holy shit, babe. There must be thousands of dollars in this bag. Can we keep it?"

"You read his note. He wants us to have it." Trish waved the money in the air. "It sure stinks, but who cares?"

Mr. C, their elderly neighbor, had pinned the cryptic note to the bag and left it in a corner of his bedroom. Trish found it when she let herself into his apartment to check on him. He'd died during the night. Fortunately, the undertakers who came for his body didn't notice it.

Trish stretched her arm as far as it would go several more times and still didn't hit bare canvas. "We should count this."

For the next hour, they stacked the money in piles of a thousand dollars each, covering every surface in the living room and the dinette table and chairs.

"You know, Trish, I got a bad feeling about this money. I mean, what if it's stolen or something? I saw on TV how the police mark the bills so if somebody spends them, they can trace the money back to them. I'd rather stay poor than end up in jail."

Trish turned the duffle upside down. A couple of crumpled pieces of newspaper tumbled out with the last of the money. Trish picked them up and smoothed them out. She read, "Largest East Coast Heist Remains Unsolved" and studied a faded photo of the First National Bank of New York in Albany.

"Holy Christ, would you look at this?"

Gabby peered over Trish's shoulder. "Jesus, Maria y Jose, I told you it was hot money. We gotta call the cops. I ain't going to jail for this."

"Calm down. Nobody's going to jail. This is an old article. Look, it says July 16, 1943." Gabby paced while Trish read on. "It says the FBI has no suspects yet, even though they offered a five thousand dollar reward for information leading to the arrest and conviction of the perpetrators."

"Maybe we can claim the reward and blame it on Mr. C," Gabby joked.

"Very funny." Trish read from the second article. "The FBI admits a month has gone by with no arrests. An Albany police officer says the thieves got away with nearly two million dollars in unmarked bills and securities."

"What are securities?"

"I don't know, but it says the bills were unmarked."

"So we could spend the money and not get caught?"

"Listen to you. A minute ago you were ready to turn the money over to the cops, and now you're ready to go shopping." Trish picked a fifty off one of the piles on the dinette table and wiggled it in front of Gabby's face.

"What are you thinking? You have that wild look that makes my blood pressure skyrocket."

"I think we should have a fancy meal in a restaurant like they do after a wake. How about we go down to Dominic's and have supper in honor of Mr. C?"

Gabby struck a thoughtful pose, hand on her chin.

Uh oh, Trish thought. Here it comes. Gabby's going to get on her high horse and deliver one of her sermons. She sucked in her breath and waited.

"I feel like Chinese. Let's go to the Chop Stick Inn."

"Hah! Okay, but let's finish counting this money first. We can't leave it lying around like this."

Among the crumpled bills and clippings Trish found a photo of a man and woman with three boys on a ship. For sure, Mr. C was the youngest one. His face hadn't changed that much. She decided to frame it and put it on her nightstand.

Trish grabbed a pen and paper and counted. She tallied three times. "This can't be right. Here, you do it."

Gabby labored over her calculations for several minutes. "What'd you get?"

"Ninety-six thousand and one hundred dollars, plus the fifty in my pocket."

"Yeah, me too. Jesus, Maria y Jose, we could buy a house with this money."

"A house? We could buy this whole friggin building and a car."

"I want a red Cadillac with one of those singing horns," Gabby said.

"I can just see you pulling that baby into the diner parking lot."

"You crazy? I'm not working any more. Standing on my sore feet for eight hours, kissing asses for tips? Bullshit. I'm retiring." Gabby paused when she saw Trish's frown. "What's wrong?"

"I hope the place doesn't burn down with all this money. Where are we gonna keep it?"

Gabby rooted in the kitchen junk drawer and retrieved every elastic band she could find. They packaged the fifties and hundreds together before returning them to the black bag. Then Trish moved aside clothes and slid the bag behind garments in the back corner of the bedroom closet.

For good measure, she sprayed it with her favorite cologne, Tabu.

ON THE WAY to the bus stop, Gabby broke into hysterical laughter. She shrieked, doubled over, and tried to catch her breath. Trish laughed too, but had no idea what was so funny.

Fortunately, there was nobody else at the bus stop, and they barely managed to stop carrying on by the time the bus pulled to the curb.

"What's so funny?" Trish asked, as soon as they sat down.

"Nothing," Gabby answered, and clamped her hand over her mouth.

"You nervous?" Trish asked.

"I think I'm scared."

Trish slipped her arm around Gabby's shoulders and pulled her close enough to feel the heat of her breath. "We'll be okay. I promise."

Mr. Young, owner of the Chop Stick Inn, looked up as they entered the tiny restaurant. "Ah, ladies, good night for hot food." He picked up menus and led them to a table near the kitchen.

"You keep warm here. Too windy when door opens."

Trish inhaled deeply taking in the salty, spicy aromas that floated out of the kitchen. Hot tea erased the September chill from their walk from the bus stop. None of their usual Chow Mein that night. To celebrate, Trish chose pepper steak and Gabby tried lobster. Before leaving, Trish got an order of spare ribs "to go" in case she got hungry later and needed a snack. Or, she could eat them for breakfast after calling in sick.

"You want something to snack on?"

"No, I'm stuffed." Gabby crunched her fortune cookie open and read the little paper, "Friendship is the best gift."

Chapter Two

TRISH GLARED AT the alarm clock and groped for the button to silence it. She blinked several times to clear away the fog and was shocked to see it was five-thirty. "Where you going?"

"I'm on at seven," Gabby answered.

"Oh, big talker. I thought you were retiring."

"I am, but I feel bad leaving the girls to cover on short notice. Aren't you going in at eleven?"

"I wasn't planning to, but you're right. Why should our good luck bring them grief?"

After a few minutes, Trish padded into the bathroom. She enjoyed the warmth of the floor tiles on her bare feet. She used a towel to fan away the steam created by Gabby's shower.

"Hey, babe, I've been thinking. We shouldn't say anything to anybody about the money. If the cops find out, they'll start asking questions. I don't want any trouble."

"What reason should we give about why we're quitting? The girls will want to know."

"We can say my uncle in upstate New York died and left his house to me, and we're gonna move there and get jobs."

"But you don't have an uncle."

"I used to. He lived in Saugerties. He died when I was a kid, but nobody has to know that." A fleeting memory of Uncle Paddy in a top hat teaching her magic tricks at the family kitchen table skipped across Trish's mind. He was her favorite relative, the one who showered her with special attention and provided the unconditional love her parents couldn't.

"Yeah, good, but then we'll have to move. We can't stay here, or we'll run into the girls."

"I guess so. Our lease is up in two months. I'm sure Mrs. Donato will let us out early if we need to. If not, we can pay the lousy two months' rent."

"Where're we gonna live?" Gabby called from the shower.

"I don't know. Newark is where I lived my whole life. I don't know anyplace else."

"We could move to Puerto Rico. With that money, we could live like millionaires, and we'd have real family. My sister would love you."

"Oh sure, until she found out about us. You said they're worse about gays than the people here. Besides, I don't speak Spanish, and I hate the heat. No, forget Puerto Rico."

"I don't want to forget it. It's beautiful there. You should at least see it before you make up your mind."

"Listen, if you want to go live in Puerto Rico, take a thousand dollars and go. I'm not going."

"A lousy thousand dollars? How come I don't get half the money?" Gabby tore open the shower curtain and aimed the showerhead at Trish. Its stream soaked the walls, the floor, and towels on the rack.

"You're insane," Trish screamed. "Turn that off or you'll flood the place." She grabbed two damp towels and mopped furiously before the water could seep down to the super's apartment.

Gabby stood shivering in the tub. "I need a towel. Can you get me one, please?"

"I should let you freeze your ass off." Trish took a dry towel from the linen closet and threw it at Gabby. She continued wiping down the walls and floor. "Look at this," she said, and held up a sopping roll of toilet paper.

Gabby climbed out of the tub and, clad only in a towel, approached Trish. "You wouldn't really let me move to Puerto Rico without you, would you?"

"I wasn't serious before, but after this..."

"Come on, babe. We're not gonna break up over this money, are we? If that's what being rich means, I'll flush it all down the toilet, so help me."

"And give up your red Cadillac?"

"Yeah, I'd look like a pimp in it, anyway. But seriously, we're happy as long as we're together, right?"

"Yeah, of course. I think this money is making us both a little crazy. Let's not say anything about quitting the diner until we have a chance to think about what we're gonna do, okay?"

"I want you to promise me nothing's gonna change with us, Trish. Without you, being rich doesn't mean shit."

Trish ran her hand up Gabby's wet arm, stroked her neck, and rested a hand on her cheek. She kissed her and said, "I love you, babe. Don't worry. We'll work it out. Go get ready for work."

Gabby hated leaving in the dark. They'd just turned the clocks back a week earlier and the early darkness and colder morning temperatures made it harder to kick-start the day.

After a leisurely breakfast of Sanka and challah toast, Trish ironed her uniform. She loved the smell of ironing; the steam coaxed the fresh scent of laundry detergent from the nylon fabric. The smell reminded her of Mr. C. He always smelled like crisp linen, with a hint of starch. Even during the humid summers, he wore a freshly pressed, long-sleeved white shirt. One day, when he rolled up his sleeve and showed her an ugly scar reaching from his wrist to his inner elbow, she understood why.

The steam from Gabby's shower had dissipated, but streaks remained on the mirror over the sink. The familiar clanging of the pipes signaled that Mrs. Donato had turned on the heat. The law said she didn't have to provide heat until September 30, but she had a good heart and liked to keep her tenants happy.

AT THE END of her eight-hour shift, Trish dragged her body to the bus stop. She felt relieved to sink into the worn leather seat behind the bus driver and slip off her shoes. She massaged her aching feet and thought of how nice it would be to break this routine. Thoughts of Mr. C's money, and imminent retirement from the daily drudgery, made the time pass quickly.

During the past couple of days, excitement about the money in the black bag had pushed most other thoughts out of her mind. While walking from the bus stop to her building, she suddenly remembered the letter Mr. C had given her months earlier, with instructions to open it only after his death. She rushed into the building and hurried down the hall, her heart rate quickened as she unlocked the door.

Gabby was watching TV in the living room when Trish raced into the bedroom and tore open the closet door. "What did you do with the shoeboxes I had on the top shelf of the closet?" she called in a panic.

Gabby ran into the bedroom. "What's the matter with you? Why are you yelling at me?"

"Because if you threw them out, I'm going to kill you. Did you?"

"I'm not going to talk to you until you calm down. You're crazy." Muttering in Spanish, Gabby returned to the living room and turned the TV back on.

Trish stormed after her. She switched off the TV before a picture formed on the crackling screen, and planted herself in front of Gabby. "I had a very important letter in the box with the green sandals. I have to find it."

Gabby tried to maneuver around Trish, but Trish stood her ground.

"Do you want me to show you where I put your precious sandals or not? You said they don't even fit anymore. I don't know why you need to keep them."

Trish shadowed Gabby back to the bedroom and watched as she pointed to the shoe hanger on the inside of the closet door. Gabby lifted the green sandals from a pocket and dangled them by the straps. "Are these what you're looking for?"

"Where's the box they were in?" Trish demanded, through clenched teeth.

"I threw it out when we got the shoe hanger. I told you I was making room on the top shelf of the closet. If you'd listen to me, maybe you'd hear things when I tell you."

Trish sank to the bed and put her head in her hands. When Gabby swung the sandals in front of her, Trish looked up long enough to swat them away.

"I found the goddamned shoes. What the hell is wrong with you?"

"There was a letter from Mr. C in the box," Trish whispered.

"I didn't see any letter. The only thing in the boxes I got rid of was tissue paper, and I put it in the bag where we keep wrapping paper."

Trish remembered what Mr. C had told her. "You don't show this to nobody. You open it after I'm dead." The room seemed to shrink, and Trish felt faint.

Gabby tossed the shopping bag full of tissue paper onto the bed next to Trish. "See? This is all that was in those boxes." She left the room.

"Where'd you put those boxes?" Trish yelled.

"In the garbage."

"In the garbage where?" Trish hoped Gabby might have put them in the basement and that, by some miracle, they'd still be there.

Trish knocked the bag off the bed, spilling the contents all over the bedroom floor. When she bent to retrieve the tissue paper, she saw the envelope. Clasping it to her chest, she sobbed.

Gabby ran into the bedroom. "Are you all right? I think you need a doctor."

Her throat choked with emotion, Trish waved the letter at her.

"Oh, good. Now, can you start acting like a normal person? You scared the shit out of me. I thought you were having a nervous breakdown. What's so important about that letter?"

"I don't know, but Mr. C said it was important, and I shouldn't open it till he was dead."

"So, open it. Is it safe for me to bring you a knife?"

"Don't need one." When Trish slipped her finger under the flap, the red sealing wax cracked and scattered all over the floor. Her hands shook as she read the letter to herself. "Sit with me," she patted the bed next to her. "Can you read this?"

"You read. I don't have my glasses."

"Dear Patricia, I'm sorry I never told you about my life except the vendetta that followed me to New York. My life was nothing much. Weekend operas on the radio, watching TV, and eating Dominic's food by myself. You and Gabriella are the only ones who ever paid attention to me. I never said it because I didn't want you to get the wrong idea, but I love you like family."

Gabby, now also in tears said, "Oh, the poor man. What a way to live." She got up and returned with a box of tissues. "What vendetta?"

"Oh, nothing. Some kid beat him up in Sicily and he got even. Then, years later, the kid's two brothers showed up in Gloversville and wanted Mr. C to help them rob a bank or they said they'd harm his family. Crazy guy stuff. When he told me, it sounded like he borrowed it from a movie. He said that Sicilians are big on revenge. Don't worry about it."

Trish continued. "If you're reading this, I must be dead. Thank you for taking care of things with Caruso's and the apartment. I'm a very rich man, but I have nobody to leave anything to. I want you girls to have the money that's left."

"He must mean the money in the black bag."

"Wait, there's more," Trish said. She flipped the letter over.

"You have to go to the cemetery in Gloversville to get the money, but be careful. Don't tell anybody where you're going and make sure nobody follows you. There are people who would kill for it."

"A cemetery?"

"Yeah, it's where Mr. C's buried with his family. The undertaker told me that's what he arranged."

"Holy shit, Trish. Maybe he did rob a bank."

"Be quiet and listen." Trish continued to read. "On the next page is a map of the cemetery so you can find the money. Remember the name Tredita. It means three fingers in Italian. That's where the money is. Please remember me the way you knew me, and keep close to the Holy Spirit. With respect and love, Nicolo."

"You were right," Gabby said. "That was his real name."

Trish turned the map to view it from every angle. "He must have thought I was a friggin magician to follow this chicken scratch.

"Does it say the name of the cemetery?"

"Nothing."

"Maybe there's only one cemetery in the town. What's that stuff about the Holy Spirit? Did he think you were religious?"

"No way. He knew I had no use for the church, and neither did he. Maybe he meant it to be funny. He always joked about going to church."

Gabby's voice climbed an octave. "Is somebody gonna try to kill us? I don't like the sound of this. I think we should call the cops. We have enough money with the black bag."

"Let me think about it. We don't have to do anything right away." Trish pulled Gabby to her. "I promise I won't do anything to put us in danger. Nothing's worth risking our lives."

"Then let's call the cops."

"No. No cops. If we showed them the letter, you think they wouldn't try to find the money and keep it for themselves? You know I'm right."

They walked into the kitchen and Gabby climbed onto a stepladder to reach the cabinet on top of the fridge, a location she thought about often. She handed one of two dusty bottles of Four Roses to Trish. "I don't know about you, but I'm gonna be looking over my shoulder wherever I go." Gabby poured half a juice glass for each of them.

Trish raised her glass. "To our good health."

Gabby looked into Trish's eyes for several seconds before she said, "Amen," and drained her glass.

Chapter Three

One night during a lull in the late shift at Scotty's Diner, Trish asked her close friend, Rosalie, "Those two guys who come in here every couple of nights...the ones with the nice suits who leave big tips... Are they really gangsters? I hear them talking about whacking people. They beat people up for real?"

"You mean Vincent and Little Carmine, the *goombahs*? Of course they're serious." Rosalie put an arm around Trish's shoulders and whispered, "Whacking doesn't mean beating people; it means killing them. The reason they never take their suit jackets off is cause they're packing heat."

Trish wrinkled her brow. "Heat?"

"Guns. Once in a while, if you see them reach for the sugar or ketchup, you can see a bulge under their arms. Haven't you ever seen a shoulder holster?"

"Where would I see one?"

"Be nice to those guys. You might need them sometime. They've done me a few favors."

Trish didn't have to wait long to find out how rough the goombahs could be. A few nights later, a man came in and staggered to a booth in Trish's station. When she walked over to take his order, the smell of whiskey was so strong, she took a step back. He could hardly keep his eyes open as he ordered pie and coffee. Prompted by past experiences of cleaning up puke, Trish quickly brought his order. After she set his coffee on the table, he grabbed her butt and she slapped his hand away.

"Look, mister. I don't want to make a federal case out of this, but if you don't behave, I'll have to tell the owner, and he might hurt you."

Trish ducked into the kitchen and Rosalie watched Vincent approach the drunk's table.

"Jesus, you'd a thought he tore off Trish's clothes and tried to rape her," she told the girls later. "Vincent, Mr. Protector, dragged the guy out of his seat and took him out into the vestibule. I couldn't hear what he said to him, but he jammed him up against the cigarette machine and never let go of his collar. Next thing I know, they're back inside, and the big shot tells me to get Trish. The drunk looked so green I thought he was gonna barf."

Trish picked up the next part of the story. "Vincent took me over to the drunk. 'Tell her,' he said. I thought the guy was going to piss himself. I almost felt sorry for the poor bastard."

"Sorry? He had it coming," Carla said.

"The guy says, 'I'm sorry, miss. I apologize. I didn't mean no disrespect.' Slobber ran out of his nose and mouth. 'I swear to God. Please forgive me,' he mumbled half-crying. I worried they might kill him. Vincent told the guy, 'Get your shit and get the hell out of here, and don't let me see you here no more.'"

Trish drew a wrinkled twenty out of her pocket. "He tossed this on the table as he bolted for the register. Not a bad tip for pie and coffee," she said.

When Trish went over to Vincent's table to thank him, he said, "That scum ever shows his face around here again, you let me know. You don't have to take that from anybody."

"What's going on?" Trish's boss asked, the next time she was in the kitchen.

"It's okay. The guy had a snoot full and got smart. The goom-bahs took care of the creep. They always look out for us girls."

Later that night, Trish saw her boss standing outside the diner watching her walk to the bus stop. She waved as she got on the bus.

GABBY DOZED IN the weathered armchair with her stock-inged feet propped on the coffee table. Trish tiptoed into the kitchen, but her coat sleeve caught on the back of a dinette chair and dragged it across the parquet floor.

"Oh, hi babe," Gabby called. "I must've been sleeping. Rosa-lie called before. She said to ask you about your exciting night with the goombahs. What happened?"

Trish recounted the scene with the drunk, and Gabby laughed picturing the event.

Trish pulled the drunk's twenty out of her pocket. "This will make a nice dent in the rent that's due at the end of the week."

"Yeah, and you don't have to scream at me this time cause I'm short. Just haul one of those smelly bills out of the black bag.

I'm happy we don't have to fight about money anymore, babe," Gabby said, and put her arms around Trish's waist.

"No, all we have to worry about is digging up a dead body in some cemetery to find more money. Do you ever wish we could go back to just fighting about the rent money? Whoever thought being rich would be so complicated?"

TRISH RECALLED THE first time rent was due after Gabby moved in. She had worried the whole way home about confronting her because Gabby probably didn't have the money. Her steps quickened as she approached the apartment door. The smells of Gabby's onions, garlic and peppers teased her nose the closer she got.

Although supper was tempting, after pushing her rice and beans around the plate, Trish put her fork down.

"You're not eating," Gabby said. "Don't you like it?"

"You know what tomorrow is?" Trish asked.

Gabby looked down for several seconds before saying, "I know, I thought I'd have my share, but I sent extra to my family this month. My father missed a few days of work when he was sick."

Trish dug her nails into her palms and fought to control her voice. "Gabby, I'm real proud of you for helping your parents. I wouldn't piss on mine if they were on fire, but if you send so much to San Juan, how're you going to come up with your share of expenses? It's not fair to me."

Over the next few hours, two plates full of food went into the garbage, Gabby shrieked in Spanish and English fearful that Trish was throwing her out, and in a fit of rage picked up a snow globe of the Empire State Building and raised it over her head.

"Put that down. My sister gave it to me. It's the only thing I have from home."

Gabby backed away from Trish and put the globe down.

"I'm not throwing you out, Gabby. Let's sit and figure this thing out." She reached for Gabby's hand and held firm when Gabby tried to wrench it away.

Trish wiped muddy mascara off Gabby's cheeks. She leaned over and kissed her wet face but pulled back when Gabby returned the kiss with intensity.

"Oh, no. I know your tricks. We're not going to make love till we resolve this."

They agreed Gabby would give Trish money each week from her tips and not have to hand over so much at the end of the month.

That settled, Gabby rose to her full five feet six inches and growled, "Come over here, you. I want to make love to you." She pushed Trish down on the couch, leaning over to let her curls cover Trish's face. While she smothered her neck and shoulders with nips and kisses, she worked her knee between Trish's legs and began moving it up and down, putting pressure on her sweet spot.

"Ooh, that's nice. Is that my favorite leg?"

"No, it's the other one."

With one hand, Gabby undid the button on Trish's slacks and reached for the place where her knee was already working moist magic. Her other hand kneaded Trish's breasts, gently at first, then tweaking her erect nipples through her bra.

Trish reached around and unhooked her bra with barely a minute to spare. She squeezed her eyes shut and let the tension from every muscle in her body carry her to the brink and consume her.

Gabby collapsed on top of Trish and lay listening to her heart slow from a gallop to an easy trot.

"Oh, Gabby. You could make me believe in God again."

Trish ended up borrowing forty dollars from Mr. C. the next day and nearly choked when he tried to give her a fistful of large bills. It was not the last argument over money they would have, but Trish refused to take anything from him that she couldn't pay back. How does a guy like him get that kind of money? she wondered. The black duffel changed all that.

THE NEXT NIGHT, Gabby returned from work carrying a bag from Snyder's Hardware and put it on the dinette table.

"What's that?" Trish asked.

"Something to help us sleep better."

Trish peeked into the bag and saw a Crime Buster chain lock. "We already have two chain locks. What do we need this for?"

"The salesman said this is absolutely burglar-proof. In case somebody tries to break in to steal the money, this will make them think twice. He said it would take a power saw to break it."

Trish admitted, "I thought it was just me. I feel like I sleep with one eye open lately."

Even at work, she knew she hadn't done a great job of concealing her anxiety when Rosalie asked, "You okay? You seem a little weirder than usual today."

"I'm okay. I got a call about my Uncle Paddy in Saugerties saying he's got cancer. He's not doing too good, and I'm worried about him."

"I'm sorry. What's his last name? I'll say a prayer for him."

"Mulkern, same as mine. Thanks."

Trish related the conversation to Gabby that night. "Let's stick with that story in case somebody else asks."

"Don't you feel like a shit lying to a good friend?"

"Of course I do. I feel strange all the time lately, like I'm in somebody else's head. I'm glad I picked up a couple of extra shifts. When I'm working, I feel more normal. No time to think. As soon as I come home, the weirdness starts up. You?"

"You know me. I'm still worried somebody will break in one night and murder us to get the money." She held out her left hand to display nails chewed down to the quick.

AFTER A FEW weeks, things seemed to calm down. They agreed to shelve talk about going to Gloversville for now and Trish slept more soundly. Gabby's nails grew, and she resumed humming to Latin music on the Spanish radio station, a habit that used to annoy Trish but now seemed strangely reassuring.

Lulled into a false sense of normalcy, Trish dragged herself into the building after a double shift and was surprised when Gabby opened the door before she put her key in the lock. Gabby's eyes were wide open, and her face and neck were flushed.

"Who died?" Trish asked. "Is everything okay in San Juan?"

"Get in here," Gabby said, and pulled Trish into the apartment before engaging the dead bolt and slipping the chain locks into place. "You got a call."

Thinking that someone in her own family had died, Trish's pain resurfaced as she briefly recalled her father throwing her out of the house when she was eighteen. For several weeks after, she'd tried to stay connected to the youngest ones by stopping at their school during recess and talking to them through the fence. When she asked about the source of the telltale bruises on their faces and arms, like most kids, they readily spilled details about their mother punching them whenever they brought up Trish's name. Knowing it was merely a matter of time before her parents poisoned them against her, and not wanting to cause them further harm, she quit trying to see them.

"From who?" she asked, trying to imagine which of her parents might have died.

"Some guy with an accent asked for you. Jesus, Maria y Jose." Gabby's words came in bursts like her breath. "He said Patricia, not Trish. You know I don't believe in ghosts, but I swear to God he sounded just like Mr. C. When I asked his name, he wouldn't tell me. After I said you weren't here, he said he'd call back."

Trish dropped her purse to the floor and put her arms around Gabby to stop her from shaking. "It's all right, babe. Last I heard, ghosts don't make phone calls. Half the old people in this neighborhood have accents like Mr. C's. It's probably somebody selling something. I'm sure it's nothing."

Gabby muttered, "Jesus, Maria y Jose" several more times and peered into Trish's eyes. "I think we should call the cops."

"No, no cops. You have to trust my judgment. I know I'm right."

Trish felt sweat trickle down her sides from her armpits and walked to the wall thermostat. It must be my nerves, she thought. It's only seventy degrees in here. Calming Gabby was her first priority. She hoped if she reassured her lover enough times, she'd believe it herself. What if those Sicilian guys who were after Mr. C found out he died? If they knew he had a friend, would they think she could lead them to his money?

Trish had developed a habit of pushing aside clothes to be sure the black bag was undisturbed each time she opened the bedroom closet. Some days she even talked to it as if she could coax the secret source of the money out of the canvas fibers. Each time she unzipped the bag, she felt slightly queasy when the musty smell rushed up her nostrils.

OVER SUPPER ONE night a few weeks later, Gabby admitted, "You were right about that phone call. It was nothing. It probably was a salesman."

Later, while watching TV, Gabby slid over to Trish and rubbed her shoulders where she stored up all of life's aggravation. Carrying heavy trays at work took its toll on her body. Trish "oohed" and "aahed." When she turned so Gabby could massage her entire back, she felt a hand slip around under her arm and land on her breast. Gabby caressed her nipple.

"Ooh, that's nice." It was one of those nights when they'd miss the eleven o'clock news, and Trish didn't care.

Chapter Four

LATER THAT WEEK, when the late afternoon light cast a golden glow over the stucco-and-tan brick row houses on her block, Trish walked slowly as she approached her building. It was tricky dodging acorns that dive-bombed from the old oaks lining the street. She inhaled deeply and appreciated the crisp snap in the air while her eyes soaked up the vibrant colors of the leaves that sheltered in the corners of the front steps. Mail was sparse that day, and she let herself into the apartment. Slipping out of her uniform, she thought she heard a knock at the door.

"Who is it?" She stretched to look through the peephole.

"It's your neighbor, Esther."

"Hang on a sec. Let me grab a robe."

Trish clutched her yellow chenille robe closed, fastened the top snap and tied the belt. She opened the chains and released the deadbolt.

"Come on in, Esther."

Esther took a few tentative steps into the apartment and stopped. "I probably should mind my own business..."

That would be a first, Trish thought.

"You want a cup of coffee? I was just gonna have some. It's instant, if you don't mind. Gabby made cookies yesterday. Have a seat. It won't take long."

"I can't stay long. You got a nice place here."

"Thanks. You never been in here?"

"I don't think so." She wandered into the living room. "Good-looking family."

Trish knew she must be looking at a photo of Gabby's family. Nobody in Trish's family could quit fighting long enough to pose for a group picture. Even if they had, she wouldn't want to put it in the apartment.

"Yeah, that's Gabby's family. Her father's a hunk, isn't he?"

Trish poured coffee and stirred sugar into her mug. "So, what's up?"

"Well, the other day I came into the building and stopped at my mailbox. There was a guy there studying the boxes, so I asked if I could help him. He said he was looking for Patricia."

Trish's hand stopped in mid-stir.

"You're the only Patricia I know in the building, so I asked what her last name was. He seemed jumpy and when he said he didn't know it, I got suspicious. Then I did a stupid thing. I should have known better."

Trish's muscles stiffened, and her mind flashed back to the phone call Gabby took.

"I told him the only Patricia I knew was Patricia Mulkern."

"Yeah," he said. "That's her."

"You know how you can tell when some people are lying? He was twitching his fingers back and forth like this. He told me he met you and thought you were very nice, but he was too shy to ask for your number, so he was trying to find out where you live."

"What'd he look like?"

"Not bad looking. Maybe five eight or nine and he had dark eyes, kind of greenish brown. His hair was salt-and-pepper colored and curly. It was long in the back curling over his jacket collar. If I had to guess, I'd say he was Italian. He looked a lot older than you, though."

"Did he have an accent?"

Esther shook her head from side to side.

"It doesn't sound like anybody I know," Trish said, and tilted her chair back to see if she'd fastened the chain locks.

"Here's the really odd thing. I figured on the off chance that he was telling the truth, maybe he needed some encouragement, so I reached in front of him and pushed your doorbell. He shouted, 'W-w-what d-d-did you d-d-do?' I told him I rang your bell, and he wheeled and ran out the door. I followed him out and watched him run up the street and jump into a black car with out-of-state plates. He pulled out right in front of a bus. The bus screeched its brakes and just missed hitting him."

Too bad, Trish thought. She drank her coffee while Esther talked and tried not to show her concern. She hoped it wasn't the same guy who called.

"I don't want to cause trouble for you. I wasn't gonna say anything, but I figured you'd want to know."

"No, you did the right thing. I'm glad you told me. It's probably someone from the diner. Sometimes, guys try to find out where the waitresses live. It happens to the other girls from time to time, too. That's probably who it was."

Trish made it a practice not to discuss her relationship with Gabby. Some of the girls at the diner knew, but other than them, Mr. C was the only one she told. People in her building had a 'live and let live' policy. She didn't ask what went on in the other tenants' apartments, and they didn't ask what happened in hers.

"I was kind of surprised a guy was looking for you with you and Gabby...you know."

Keep fishing, Esther.

"I'm not so bad to look at," Trish said, smiling. "Some guys go for chunky women. More to grab onto." She cupped her hands under her breasts.

Esther's eyes widened and no sound came from her open mouth. Finally, after a long pause, she got up. "Gotta go. My clothes are in the dryer. Thanks for the coffee and cookies."

"YOU OKAY?" GABBY asked, when Trish picked up the phone.

"Yeah, why do you ask?"

"You know me. My Puerto Rican ESP just kicked in, so I needed to check. You sure you're okay?"

"Yeah," Trish lied. When you coming home?"

"Just having a bite with the girls. Want me to bring you something?"

"Nope. Got leftovers. See you soon." Trish barely got the words out before the dime dropped and the line went dead on the diner phone.

TRISH PACED FROM the bedroom, to the living room, and into the kitchen trying to figure out the best way to tell Gabby about what Esther saw.

"Did you miss me?" Gabby said, when she got home. She reached for a hug with the free arm that wasn't weighed down with her ten-pound shoulder bag, and reacted when Trish stiffened. "I knew something was wrong. What is it?"

"We gotta talk, babe."

"Now what? You lose another pair of shoes? Whatever's missing this time, it's not my fault. I had a shitty day at work. Must be a full moon. Every lunatic in Newark ended up at my station. Make that poor lunatics. Tips stunk. So, whatever you want to blame me for, save it. I'm not in the mood."

"Whoa, babe. You came in here with horns and now I'm public enemy number one? You getting a split personality?"

Gabby laughed. "You know how I get when it's my 'time of the month.' I'm sorry. Maybe I'm the lunatic today. What's up?"

"Come sit. We have a problem. No, get those wrinkles off your forehead; it's not a 'you-and-me' problem."

Trish related Esther's story and Gabby's frown lines deepened. "You should have seen the look on Esther's face when I suggested a guy was interested in me. It was worth a million, like somebody zapped her with a ray gun. I don't mind if she's confused."

Gabby didn't comment because she was halfway to the bedroom. She returned carrying a suitcase.

"You going somewhere?" Trish asked.

"It's not safe to stay here. I don't know who this guy is, but whoever he is, I don't want to hang around until he kills you."

"Maybe what I told Esther is true. He could be trying to hit on me."

"Uh-uh. My gut tells me he's trouble, and we'd better get out of here for a few days. We always wanted to go to Cape May. We can use some of Mr. C's money."

"Nobody goes down the shore in October. We'll freeze our asses off."

"So, we'll bring coats."

Trish crinkled her nose and tilted her head at an angle.

"Fine. If you want to stay here and be a sitting duck, do it. When I come back, I'll give you a nice funeral."

Trish punched Gabby's arm. "You'd leave me here to get murdered?"

She listened as Gabby phoned Rosalie. "We got a family emergency. Tell the boss to get somebody to cover for us over the weekend, too. We should be back by Monday."

"You don't really think this guy wants to kill me, do you?" Trish asked, trying to ignore the lump in her throat.

"I'm sure as hell not willing to stay around to find out. Are you? Come on, let's pack."

Trish took cash from the black bag and returned it to its hiding place. "Think three hundred's enough?"

"That's like eight weeks' pay for me. You took fifties, right? We'd get mugged if we tried to cash a hundred."

THE NEXT MORNING, they took a bus to Penn Station, loaded up with sandwiches from the station deli, and boarded a bus. Not wanting to get off during stops at Camden and Philadelphia carrying that much money, they managed to control their swelling bladders until the bus pulled in to the welcome center in Cape May.

They checked into a Victorian bed and breakfast with pink gingerbread trim, a block from the ocean. A couple of hours in separate beds was Trish's limit before she crawled in with Gabby in the middle of the night. At breakfast, two middle-aged men seated at the table across from them smiled knowingly.

Heading toward the ocean, Gabby inhaled deeply and smiled. "Reminds me of Puerto Rico. I love the salty air." She closed her eyes and imagined palm trees and bougainvillea.

Walking along the deserted beach, Gabby reached for Trish's hand. "Why not?" she asked after Trish pulled away. "Nobody here knows us. They'll think we're sisters."

Trish laughed. "Sure, we look so much alike. You're right, though." She intertwined her fingers with Gabby's.

As they neared the surf, Trish broke away and ran toward the water. She sat to remove her socks and shoes and roll up her pant legs.

"What're you doing?"

"Wading. Come on."

They held hands and walked into the water, watching the sand swirl around their feet, and wobbled as they sank deeper with each step. The water seemed remarkably warm compared to the brisk air. For the moment, it was just the two of them. No Newark, no creepy guy. Relaxation washed over them. Trish spread her arms out and inhaled the ocean air. She dipped and swayed, mimicking the gulls that swooped in and out of the water.

"I HAVEN'T SEEN you smile this much in months," Gabby said at lunch on their third day in Cape May.

The smile faded when Trish tried to pay the check with a fifty.

"I can't change that for you, but you can go down the street to the bank," the waitress said.

"I'll stay till she comes back," Gabby offered.

"You don't have to. I trust you."

Trish and Gabby laughed.

"What's so funny?"

"We're not used to anybody trusting anyone. We're from Newark," Gabby said.

"Oh, yeah. I hear it's a rough place. Never been there."

"Not really. Most people are very nice, but you do have to be careful of rip-off artists," Trish replied.

Trish returned from the bank, paid the check, and left a generous tip before they sauntered along the pedestrian promenade looking for a tourist trap to buy souvenirs.

"THAT'S THE FIRST vacation I ever had," Trish said, as they settled into their seats for the return trip. "I bet I've gained five pounds. I felt it as I hoisted myself up the steps."

"If we lived in Puerto Rico, we'd be on vacation all the time," Gabby remarked.

Trish glanced at her sideways and sneered. The bus chugged up the Garden State Parkway and switched to the New Jersey Turnpike, near Edison. The closer they got to Newark, it felt like a giant eraser wiped away their relaxed mood. Gabby slept most of the way and Trish, despite trying to keep her mind on the beach, returned to thoughts of the creepy guy. She watched the scenery turn grayer and smelled fumes from the refineries as they passed through Elizabeth. Snaking through downtown Newark, Trish felt her mood darken to match the grubby buildings on either side of the road.

With Penn Station in sight, she woke Gabby and said, "The problem with going someplace beautiful is that it's so depressing coming home." She reached for their suitcase in the overhead luggage rack and felt in her pocket for her keys. Once off the bus, she arranged the keys between the knuckles of her free hand, a habit so ingrained she couldn't recall when she'd first learned it.

Chapter Five

"I GUESS I'M NOT a very good liar," Gabby said. "I feel like I'm inside a giant, over-inflated balloon waiting for it to pop. Every time I lie to somebody, I feel like they know it."

"I've almost slipped a couple times," Trish said. "At least we still know when we're lying. If we start believing our own bullshit, we're in real trouble."

On their first morning back at work, Trish and Gabby hadn't even taken their coats off yet when three of the waitresses rushed over to them. One asked, "Rosalie told us you have a sick uncle. Is that why you had to go out of town?"

"Yeah, Uncle Paddy's got cancer. One minute, the poor guy's going down fast and then, within hours, he rallies."

"You were very slick with the story of your uncle's miraculous retreat from death's door," Gabby said, when they had a minute to review the day's events.

"I have a stabbing pain right here every time I lie," Trish said, pointing to her head. "Is it possible for your conscience to hurt? I think Uncle Paddy's gonna have more lives than a cat by the time we get out of here."

Over supper a few nights after they returned, Gabby asked, "Do you think that guy came back while we were gone?"

"With Esther Swirsky on the case? I'm sure we'd have heard by now. I saw her the day after we got back, and she didn't say anything. You ever know her to miss out on a chance to deliver news? She did say the mailman told her we hadn't picked up our mail, so I told her we took a small vacation."

"Maybe we should put up a chart so we can keep track of what lies we tell to which person," Gabby suggested. "I'm afraid I'm going to screw up."

WITH A WEEK to go before Halloween, the diner took on a festive look with orange and black crepe paper and black cutouts of witches on broomsticks, cats with arched backs, and dancing silver skeletons. Decorating seemed to put customers in a holiday mood and, though nobody had hard scientific proof, the waitresses insisted tips got better.

Gabby looked forward to seeing the neighborhood kids in costumes and stocked up on bags of candy. Trish worked out the diner schedule so Gabby could have off that night. "Remember, no scary mask," she cautioned, before leaving for work. She recalled the time Gabby's Frankenstein mask frightened a little girl so badly that the kid's mother called her a bitch and took a swing at her. On her way to work, Trish watched younger kids parade down the street in their ghost and hobo costumes, two favorites in the poorer neighborhoods. It made the bus ride go faster and tweaked a distant memory of helping her younger sisters prepare for the big night.

TRISH WORKED UNTIL eleven that night and felt drained from giving out orange-and-black iced cupcakes to every kid who showed up in a costume. As she approached her apartment, she noticed pieces of candy on the hall floor and thought to herself that some ungrateful kids probably tossed the ones they didn't like. Knowing Gabby would wait up for her, she knocked on the door. When Gabby didn't answer, she tried her key and found the chain locks engaged.

"Goddammit." She tried inserting her finger but couldn't move the chains. "Gabby, quit fooling around and open the door."

Trish's chest tightened and she sucked in her breath when she saw a man open the front door and start down the hall toward her. At first, she didn't recognize her upstairs neighbor, Eddie O'Donnell, because he wore a hat with the brim tugged down over his eyes.

"Are you locked out?"

"Yeah, Gabby must've put the chains on and fallen asleep. I don't want to wake the whole building by yelling, but I don't know what to do."

"Give me your number. I'll call and wake her."

"Humboldt four, four eight four two. Thanks, Eddie. Let it ring till she answers." Trish watched him take the steps two at a time and heard his door open and shut.

After eight or nine rings, Gabby awoke and heard someone banging on the door. Seeing Trish through the peephole, she opened the door. "Who the hell is calling this late?" she snarled and rubbed sleep from her eyes.

Trish pushed past her and answered the phone. "Yeah, it worked. Thanks a million."

"Who was that?"

"Eddie O'Donnell. If it wasn't for him, I'd have been spending the night in the hall. Why'd you put the chains on?"

"I'm sorry, babe. I can't believe I fell asleep on the couch. It's been a rough night. We gotta move out of here."

Trish put her purse on a chair and took off her raincoat. "Mind telling me why we have to move?"

"I met him tonight."

"I'm too tired for games, babe. Who'd you meet?"

"The guy who's trying to find you. He came to the door with a mask on and thought I was you."

"Oh, Christ. How'd you know it was him?"

"It had to be him. He asked if I was Patricia, not Trish, and he said he wanted to talk to me, I mean you. And he had a thick accent."

"Calm down and tell me exactly what happened."

"I was down to my last bowl of candy when I saw what I thought was a big kid coming down the hall with only a half mask on. As he got closer, I realized he was no kid. I told him I was out of candy and started to close the door. That's when he asked if I was Patricia."

"Oh my God. Then what?"

"I threw the candy at him and slammed the door. I said if he didn't get out of here, I was gonna call the cops. I yelled through the door that I had a gun and knew how to use it. The guy said he was a friend of Nicolo's. For a minute, I forgot that was Mr. C's real name. I screamed at him that I didn't know any Nicolo and he'd better beat it."

"I'm glad you didn't call the cops. We don't need them nosing around." Picturing Gabby trying to scare the guy, she couldn't suppress a laugh.

"You think it's funny?"

"No, but I'm trying to imagine him when you said you'd shoot him. Did he say anything else?"

"What'd you want him to say, 'Nice to meet you' after that?"

"Okay, don't get bent out of shape. I was just asking."

"He must not know what you look like if he thought I was you," Gabby said.

"That's good." Trish took Gabby in her arms and held her. "No wonder you barricaded the door. How could you sleep after that?"

"You know me. I can always sleep. I thought I'd take a quick rest on the couch, and that I'd hear you when you got home."

Trish started to walk to the kitchen but Gabby grabbed her arm. "That's why we have to move. It's not safe to stay here anymore."

"We'll talk about it tomorrow, babe. I'm sorry it was such a rough night." She patted Gabby's cheek. "Go get ready for bed. You're on early tomorrow. I'll tuck you in. I need to stay up for a while."

Trish nursed a cup of Sanka and tried to piece together what Gabby had told her. Mr. C said he had no friends other than them. If this guy was a close friend, why didn't Mr. C leave him the money? If he was up to no good, why would he be so open about trying to find her? Then again, he lied to Esther. Of course, all this puzzling might be a waste of energy. Gabby might have scared him off for good.

"GRAB THIS AND pull it toward you slowly. I don't want to tear it."

Gabby straightened the New York/New Jersey map so they could see all of New York State spread out on the dinette table. Trish moved her finger from the New Jersey border and traced north along the New York Thruway and up the Hudson River Valley. Beyond Albany, she followed another river to Rotterdam, and then Amsterdam.

"You'd think this was a map of Holland," she said. "I remember the first time I came across names like these. Hans Brinker lived in Amsterdam. I always dreamed one day I'd be able to ice skate like those kids, but the only time I tried it in Branch Brook Park, I fell on my ass. Two of my friends managed to quit laughing long enough to help me up." She patted her butt. "Even with all this padding, I was sore for a week."

Trish continued moving her finger in wider circles until the numbers and letters on the edge of the map indicated she'd found Gloversville. "Ah, here it is."

Gabby scooted over to Trish's side of the map. Squinting, she asked, "Where? I don't see it."

"Follow my finger. Here's where we are, in Newark. The bus goes up this way on the New York Thruway. Keep watching my finger." She moved it to the tiny circle next to the name, Gloversville.

"That's not too far, only about seven or eight inches."

"Yeah," Trish laughed, "but you wouldn't want to walk it."

"What's that big lake near it?" Gabby asked.

"Lake Sacandaga."

"Sounds Indian. Do you think there are Indians there?"

Seeing Gabby's wide-open eyes and knowing her fascination for TV westerns, Trish hastened to reassure her that if there were any, they wouldn't look like the ones on TV.

"Can we get there by bus?" Gabby asked.

"Yeah, I checked. It only takes a few hours. It's closer than Cape May. We could take a ride up there and look around a little. We don't have to do anything."

"You know I hate cemeteries. We won't go into one, right?"

"I just want to see where it is. I promise you don't have to go in it."

"Can we wait a while?"

"Sure. There's no rush." She reached for Gabby's arm and patted it. "Relax, babe. I only wanted to get an idea where Gloversville is."

ONE AFTERNOON THE following week, Gabby brought in the mail and tossed it on the table without checking it. Later that evening, Trish absently flipped through several envelopes and recognized bills. She was about to leave them where they lay when she saw a handwritten envelope addressed to her. The printing looked like a child's, and out of habit she turned it over to see if there was a return address. Someone had written Ignazzio Guarino with a Gloversville, New York address.

"Oh hell, here we go again," she said, as she slit open the envelope and read, "Dear Miss Mulkern." She read the letter twice.

"Hey babe, c'mere," she called, "I got a pen pal in Gloversville."

Rushing out of the bathroom, Gabby asked, "Did you say what I thought you said?"

"Here, read this."

"There's blood on it."

"Damn! I got a paper cut." Trish sucked on her finger and went to get a Band-Aid. "Help me with this."

Gabby peeled the paper off and held the Band-Aid open while Trish extended her forefinger and Gabby wrapped it around tightly. "Squeeze it and it'll quit bleeding."

Gabby retrieved her glasses from her purse and began to read slowly. She stopped to comment, "His English is worse than mine."

"Never mind his English. What do you make of this?"

"He could be on the level. It's the same guy, for sure. Otherwise, how would he know about Halloween and the phone call? Are you gonna talk with this Guarino guy next time he calls?"

"I'm tempted. He might be able to help us, if he's telling the truth. Then, on the other hand, he could be one of those thieves who takes advantage of someone dying and tries to steal money. Did he look like a crook?"

"Well, he sure as shit wasn't the Lone Ranger with that mask on. What's a crook look like? I didn't know any crooks in Puerto Rico."

Trish and Gabby froze when they heard the unmistakable sound of someone knocking on their door.

"You go." Gabby pointed to the huge rollers claiming half her head, and the wet straight hair that contrasted with it on the other side.

TRISH TIPTOED TO the door. Instead of looking through the peephole, the way she usually did, she stood to the side. "Who is it?"

"It's me, Esther Swirsky."

"You alone?"

"No. Rock Hudson's with me."

Trish unlocked the door and invited Esther in.

"I hope I'm not interrupting anything, but I heard something and thought you'd want to know.

Trish braced herself expecting to hear about another death, except that Esther had a smile on her face. Trish explained that Gabby was indisposed.

"You're not gonna believe this," Esther began. "Margaret O'Donnell eloped yesterday." She let that bombshell lie for a minute.

Sucking in her breath, Trish exclaimed, "You are absolutely shitting me. Get outta here! Where'd you hear this?"

"Eddie told me not half an hour ago. I was carrying groceries in, and he held the door for me. I never know what to say to him, so I asked about his sister. He had the strangest look, like he was about to cry. I thought he was gonna say she died, but instead he told me she was in Atlantic City where she got married yesterday."

"Holy Christ. If ever there was a woman you'd swear would never light up anybody's dreams, Margaret's it. She's so shy, she's almost turned inside out."

Esther supplied the rest of the details she got from Eddie, including that Margaret didn't even tell him until after she got married. "She left for work in the morning like it was an ordinary day and when she called him, he thought she was calling to say she'd be late. Poor guy is in shock, I think."

Esther stood to leave and Trish imagined she was eager to make the rounds of all the tenants to spread the word. What a lucky day for her.

Eddie and his sister were old-timers in the building. They occupied the apartment directly above Trish's. Except for an occasional call to ask them to turn down their TV after ten o'clock, their only contact was when they greeted each other in the hall.

"You're not going to believe what Esther, the yenta, told me," Trish said, as she walked into the bathroom where Gabby was evening up the number of rollers on each side of her head. "Take those bobby pins out of your mouth so you don't swallow them."

"Whaaat? Is she serious?"

"Completely. Eddie told her. Esther says it's some guy from work, but they can't tell anybody from work or one of them will get fired."

Forgetting she was no longer a practicing Catholic, Gabby crossed herself. "My God, this ranks right up there with the loaves and fishes story from the Bible."

Later, in bed, Trish was unusually quiet. When Gabby began to stroke her thigh, Trish turned away.

"What's the matter, babe? Are you that upset about Margaret? Turn around."

"Not really. I'm glad for her...but...I really misjudged her. I'm usually pretty good at sizing people up, and now I'm starting to wonder. First, I was shocked to find out that Mr. C wasn't his real name and that he didn't go to his parents' or brothers' funerals. Now I find out about Margaret. Maybe I've lost my touch. How can I decide if we should trust Ignazzio Guarino if I can't rely on my gut?"

Gabby propped herself on one elbow and stroked Trish's shoulder. "This business with the money and Mr. C almost makes me sorry we knew him. We could have been happy without all this drama, right? That's what TV's for."

"Umm, sometimes I think that, too."

Chapter Six

AFTER A DAY filled with loud talk, clanging pots and pans, and juke box music cranked up to drown out all of it, Trish looked forward to a quiet evening at home. As she neared the apartment door, she felt bass vibrations through the thin soles of her shoes. Once inside, she yelled, "Will you turn that down?" No response. "Might as well talk to the goddamn wall," she muttered.

In the bedroom, Gabby danced on a throw rug to the pulsing beat of Tito Puente's music. She didn't notice Trish until she went to the record player and lifted the needle. Gabby swung around and demanded, "Why'd you do that? It was almost over."

Trish stopped the music just in time. Within seconds, Mrs. Donato banged on her ceiling, the universal signal of displeasure in apartment buildings.

"Good thing I got home just now. Do you want us to get evicted?"

"You really think she'd throw us out?"

Trish shrugged. "Do you mind doing something else tonight? I've got a lousy headache. I didn't have two minutes to take something for it. Everybody in Newark must've decided to eat out tonight." She hung up her jacket and went in search of aspirin. Foraging in the medicine chest, she nearly gave up until she moved a bottle of mouthwash and found a mostly empty Bayer bottle. She put two tablets in her mouth and scooped a handful of water from the tap to wash them down.

By the time Trish changed out of her uniform and entered the kitchen, Gabby was on the phone. Trish knew from the way she twirled the cord it wasn't the super or Ignazzio Guarino. Trish watched Gabby mark off squares on the kitchen linoleum with her bare feet.

Trish kicked off her shoes and sank into the club chair. She closed her eyes and willed the aspirin to work. Next thing she knew, Gabby touched her arm.

"Wake up, Sleeping Beauty."

Trish was surprised to see that forty minutes had elapsed. Either the nap or the aspirin had erased her headache.

Gabby had prepared *habichuelas*, one of her favorite foods. The choice of menu meant one thing; Gabby was homesick.

Trish waved the steam pouring from the aromatic dish toward her nose before tasting a few generous forkfuls. "Umm, you should make this more often, babe. It's so good."

Gabby's eyes misted over and she put down her fork. "I got a letter from my father today. My sister Elena's very sick, something with her nerves, and she falls a lot. The doctor says she won't get better and will eventually end up in a wheelchair."

"Oh my God, babe. I'm so sorry. Isn't there anything they can do?"

"Not there," Gabby answered. Through her tears, she looked intently at Trish.

"Do you want to bring Elena here?"

"Well, we have Mr. C's money. I could fly to San Juan and bring her back. It wouldn't be permanent, only until we can find a good doctor and see if he can help her. We could get a twin bed and move the dresser out into the living room, so she could sleep in the room with us."

Trish replied, "You've given this some thought, I see. Have you told her about us?"

"Well, sort of. I never used the word *lesbiana*."

"Unless she's dense, she'll see us sleeping in a bed together and figure it out. Maybe we should move some furniture out of the living room and put a bed in there for her. You're gonna have to tell her, Gabby. You can't hide it."

"But what if she won't come?"

Trish's nostrils flared, and she slammed her fork onto the table. "Hold on. Are you telling me we're willing to buy her a plane ticket, pay her medical bills, and take her in for God-knows-how-long, and she might not want to come here because we're queer?"

"Maybe."

"Well, pardon me. I'm willing to do this because she's your sister, but I'm not gonna put on an act in my own home. No way. Ain't gonna happen. What the hell's she afraid of? Does she think it's contagious?"

"It would probably only be for a few weeks, Trish. Think

about how I'd feel if she told my parents and they cut me off. Remember how you felt?"

"Can't you ask her not to tell anyone? She should be grateful that you're willing to bring her here. Surely she can keep her mouth shut, can't she?"

Instead of answering Trish, Gabby took her mostly full plate into the kitchen. Trish ate a forkful of cold beans and rice before following her.

"Don't throw it out. Put it back in the pot with mine. We'll heat it up," Trish said to Gabby, who was poised over the garbage can with her plate.

"I'm not hungry anymore," Gabby answered.

"Okay, cut the guilt trip. Look, it's our money, yours and mine. If you want to use some of it on a round-trip ticket to San Juan for yourself and one for Elena, that's fine with me, and we can use some of Mr. C's money to pay for her to see a doctor and whatever she needs, but you have to compromise."

"Compromise?" Gabby's voice soared into the top register and increased by several decibels. "You're asking me to give up my family!"

"No, I'm not. Elena should be willing to keep her trap shut if we're willing to help her."

Gabby took a deep breath. "Let me sleep on it. We can talk more tomorrow," she said, on her way out of the room.

Trish ate salad alone, and Gabby secluded herself in the bedroom. By the time Trish went in, Gabby was sound asleep. When Trish bent over and kissed her cheek, Gabby opened her eyes.

"I thought you were sleeping."

"I was, but now I want to be snuggled."

Trish undressed and climbed into bed, fitting her body around Gabby's. Within minutes, they were asleep.

THEY BOTH WORKED the early shift the next day, so there was no time to talk. While they changed out of their uniforms that afternoon, Gabby said, "Okay, I'll tell Elena about us and ask her not to say anything to our parents. I think she'll agree. I'll write her tonight."

Trish knew, given the time required for a letter to get to Puerto Rico and Elena's answer to return, it would be a couple of weeks. The impending trip to San Juan was probably why Gabby played Tito Puente's music every day. At least she didn't dance. By the time Gabby got Elena's answer, Trish was ready to tear her hair out.

EVERYTHING WAS IN place, and on a chilly, overcast day they took a bus downtown and another fume-belching one to Newark Airport. Gabby's suitcase was crammed with gifts for every member of her extended family. When Gabby exited the bus, Trish sensed something wasn't quite right with her.

Trish recognized Latin music as they neared the gate. "My God, will you look at this?"

"Oh, yeah. I forgot to tell you. People bring picnics to the airport to welcome family coming from San Juan. Watch. Here they come."

Trish looked for seats that weren't covered with picnic baskets and watched the fiesta unfold. Gabby reminded her that many families were separated for long periods of time, and that's why their arrival was so emotional. The uniformed desk clerk smiled broadly and tapped her fingers in time to the music as people embraced their relatives and friends.

"Is this how your family greets you in San Juan?"

"Oh, no. My father would never allow it. He's much too reserved."

After a half hour, people began packing up their picnic things and the woman at the desk announced that Gabby's flight would board in ten minutes.

Trish kissed Gabby on the cheek. "Have a good flight, babe. I'll pick you and Elena up on Thursday."

Gabby got in line with her ticket, and Trish watched as she and the other passengers walked into the tunnel leading to the plane. Trish marveled at how calm people were. She'd never flown and knew she'd be a nervous wreck worrying about the plane crashing. She watched the plane back away from the gate and strained to see if she could recognize Gabby in one of its small windows.

"DID GABBY GET off okay?" Rosalie asked, when Trish

arrived at the diner.

"Yeah, she's gone."

"How long will she stay in Puerto Rico?"

"She's supposed to fly back Thursday with her sister, Elena, but we don't really know how sick she is. I'm not looking forward to Gabby's sister moving in with us while she gets medical care. It's going to be really tight with three in the apartment. Please, don't say anything to Gabby."

"You can trust me. Don't sweat it. Will Gabby call to let you know what's going on?"

"Long distance? You kidding? If they're not coming back Thursday, Gabby will call herself collect and I won't accept the call. Then she'll write me with details."

Trish's brow looked permanently wrinkled and she chewed gum with a vengeance prompting Rosalie to ask, "Pardon me for saying this, Trish, but you look worried. You're not afraid Gabby will decide to stay there, are you?"

Trish closed one eye and stared at Rosalie. "You a friggin mind reader?"

Rosalie leaned over and whispered, "Your secret's safe with me." She made a zipping motion across her lips with her thumb and forefinger.

BACK IN THE apartment after her shift, Trish enjoyed the quiet. She fooled with the rabbit ears on the TV and then turned the set off, opting for total silence instead of the news. She sank into the club chair and closed her eyes. Smells from neighbors' cooking wafted in from the hallway, and she tried to identify the pungent aromas. Cabbage was a no-brainer, but the combinations of other food smells confused her. She was enjoying the first peaceful moment of the day when the phone rang. She was mildly annoyed to hear Rosalie's voice.

"Hey, I thought you might want some company with Gabby away. Want to meet at the tavern for a few drinks?"

"What about Sean?"

"Oh, he's going, too. We can hang out while he shoots pool."

"Thanks, but I'm beat. Maybe another night." Trish hoped she didn't sound obnoxious, but she didn't want to be in the same place as Rosalie's husband, especially around alcohol.

Trish abandoned the notion of silence and turned the TV back on. She sorted through the day's mail while half-listening to Douglas Edwards read the news. Her ears perked up when she heard something about Puerto Rico.

Edwards reported, "This just in to our CBS newsroom. A group of Puerto Rican nationalists scaled the White House fence and began firing at Secret Service agents. Five agents were wounded, and two Puerto Ricans were killed. Three others were taken into custody."

"My God, I can't believe this," Trish screamed at the TV.

Trish dialed Rosalie's number and shouted at her, "Turn on the news!"

"I've got it on. God, look at the dead bodies. Do you think Gabby knows about this? Do they even have TV down there? Will she be able to get back?"

TRISH NAVIGATED THE next couple of days in a fog. Except for Rosalie, she didn't discuss her fears with anybody. Rosalie pitched in and covered a couple of Trish's tables because Trish glided around the diner like a zombie. Rosalie knew it was bad when she overhead a customer ask the woman he was with if she thought their waitress was on dope. Even her regular customers didn't chat with her the way they usually did.

The boss arrived clutching a copy of the *Newark Evening News* under his arm. He approached Trish and pointed to the headline about the attack. "You think Gabby's okay? She'll be able to get back, won't she?"

"I'm sure she's fine. Don't worry about it. I expect her back soon." Her scowl belied her words.

INSTEAD OF GETTING off the bus at her usual stop that night, Trish stayed on until she recognized St. Lucy's Catholic Church. She felt like somebody else was in control of her body as she entered the church, dipped her fingers into the holy water, and made the sign of the cross. She stood at the side of the sanctuary, popped a couple of quarters from her tip money into the tin box, and selected two candles, one for herself and one for Gabby. She prayed to the Virgin Mary that Gabby would come home to her, and that nobody else would do anything crazy. At least, if they did, she prayed they wouldn't be Puerto Rican.

Trish wasn't sure if there was a God, but she figured it wouldn't hurt to pray, so she knelt in one of the front pews until her knees hurt. She looked around and realized she was the only woman in the church without a head covering. Well, no matter, God wouldn't recognize her anyway. She hadn't been in a church since she was thirteen.

BY WEDNESDAY, TRISH hadn't heard anything from Gabby and the news story about the Puerto Rican nationalists had been replaced by other crimes on the evening news. Shortly after seven, the phone rang. It was Gabby.

"Babe, I'm at Newark Airport."

"Oh, thank God. Are you okay? Is Elena with you?"

"I'm fine. No, she's not with me. I'll explain when I see you. I'm gonna grab the bus to Penn Station and then I'll catch the Number Thirteen. I should be home in about an hour and a half to two hours." The coin dropped and the phone went silent.

Without a second thought, Trish grabbed her raincoat and purse and flew out the door. She ran down the block to the bus stop and waited a few minutes until the bus screeched to a halt in front of her. Seated and looking out the window, she wondered if she'd been too hasty. What if Gabby got to Penn Station ahead of her and caught another bus? Too late to worry about it now, and besides, it was unlikely she'd get a bus from the airport so quickly. Rush hour was over and the buses didn't run that often.

With hardly any traffic, Trish's bus made it downtown in less than twenty minutes. Since there was only one way Gabby could walk from Penn Station, Trish searched the opposite side of Market Street as she walked. She claimed a spot next to the main station doors so she could survey the passengers exiting. She couldn't think of any reason why Gabby would use another exit.

Several taxis lined up where she stood and two drivers asked if she wanted a cab. She waved them off and remained glued to her vantage point. The flower seller next to her picked fresh flowers out of plastic containers as he prepared to close for the night.

"Hey, miss, I can give you a good deal if you want some flowers," he said.

"How good?"

"Pick out any six stems for a buck, and I'll throw in some Baby's Breath."

Trish chose six red roses and handed them to the seller. He added Baby's Breath and some ferns and wrapped them in wax paper, taking care to crimp the bottom so the water wouldn't leak out. Trish handed him a dollar and heard someone say, "Those better be for me."

She turned to find Gabby holding her suitcase. "Of course they're for you. Welcome home, babe. God, it's so good to see you." They stood awkwardly for a moment before Trish waved to the first taxi in line. "Come on. We're taking a cab home. I don't care how much it costs."

The yellow cab inched along the curb and Gabby pushed her suitcase in and followed it. Trish handed her the roses and slid onto the seat beside her. She pulled her trench coat under her legs and tried not to think about the stains on the seat. She leaned over to inhale the perfume of the roses that helped mask the rank odor in the taxi, most of which she guessed came from the driver.

"Thirty-six Kearny Street," she said to the back of the driver's head. He flipped the lever to start the meter and Trish took Gabby's hand and relaxed listening to the regular ticking that falsely lulled her into thinking life would return to normal.

Chapter Seven

AS SOON AS they entered the apartment, Trish grabbed Gabby and kissed her. "It feels so good to hold you again," she said, but recoiled at the smell of cigarette smoke in Gabby's hair from the plane.

"What a day," Gabby began. "The plane circled for almost an hour over Newark Airport and then, I was so excited to get home I forgot to get my suitcase from baggage claim. The bus was half-way to Penn Station when I realized it and made the driver let me off in Elizabeth. I took a taxi to the airport and got ripped off when the driver said some bullshit about an extra five dollars for going to the airport."

"Who cares? I'm so happy you came home a day early. What's five dollars? We're rich, remember. You thought I was gonna pitch a fit, didn't you?"

"Well, yeah, I thought you'd be pissed. You must have missed me plenty, huh?"

"You know how much I missed you?" Trish blurted out the story about St. Lucy's.

"Jesus, Maria y Jose," Gabby exclaimed. "You're putting me on, right? You didn't really go to church."

"Yeah, I did, and the place is still standing." Almost as an afterthought, Trish asked, "How's Elena? Why didn't she come back with you?"

A frown replaced the smile on Gabby's face. She sat down on the couch and stared straight ahead, avoiding eye contact. "I have to tell you something, and you're not gonna like it."

Oh God, Trish thought. Here it comes. Gabby's going back to her family. Every muscle in her body tensed as she prepared for the dreaded news.

"I lied about Elena. Well, I didn't lie completely. She's sick, but it's not as bad as I told you. She's anemic, and the doctors are giving her iron shots. She'll be fine in a couple of months."

"You made it sound like she was dying. Why'd you lie to me?"

Through tears, Gabby described how much she missed her family while Trish waited for the worst. "Since we have all this money now, I thought you would let me go home if I gave you a really good reason. That's why I made up the story about Elena's illness."

"So what now?"

Gabby turned to face Trish. "Can you ever forgive me? I'll never lie to you again. I swear. I've been sick about it the whole time. That's why I came back a day early."

"It's gonna take a long time before I can trust you again."

"How long?" Gabby asked.

"Why? Is there a time limit?"

"No, unless you kick me out, we have the rest of our lives. I want to make it up to you, Trish. I'm so sorry." Gabby reached for her, but Trish resisted.

"At first, I worried you'd leave me and go back to Puerto Rico, but now I wonder if I want to live with someone I can't trust." She got up. "I'm going for a walk."

"Can I come with you? It's dark out."

"No, I need some time alone."

Trish turned back before leaving the apartment and saw Gabby standing by the couch with her hands cupping her eyes. Good, she thought. Now you know how I feel.

"TROUBLE IN PARADISE?" Rosalie whispered to Trish on the first day she and Gabby worked the same shift.

Trish responded with an icy stare.

Later that night Rosalie tried again. "It's cold enough in here to freeze meat," she began, as they ate in the last booth. "I thought you'd be happy that she came back."

"I know you mean well, Ro, but butt out."

"Oh, excuse me. I was trying to be a friend. You two have been staring daggers at each other all day. I thought maybe you wanted to talk about it."

"Well, I don't. Some things are private."

Rosalie held up her hands in surrender and they finished their meal in silence. Meanwhile, Gabby busied herself filling sugar and salt-and-pepper shakers in the kitchen so she didn't have to sit with them.

At the end of the shift, Trish passed Gabby carrying her raincoat and purse. She stopped to look at Gabby and said, "I'm going home."

Gabby replied, "I might go to a movie."

ABOUT THE ONLY thing worth watching on TV that night was women's wrestling. Trish knew it was mostly fake, but she enjoyed watching powerful women fling the puny male referees out of the ring and into the audience. She changed into her pajamas and had barely settled into her chair when the phone rang.

Without thinking, Trish picked it up and heard a male voice say, "Please don't hang up. I really need to talk to you." Gabby was right. Ignazzio sounded exactly like Mr. C.

"What do you want with me?"

"I know you have no reason to trust me. I was a friend of Nicolo's in Sicily, where we grew up. I didn't see him for many years until a few months ago, when he came to Gloversville. I drove by the church and saw somebody walking into the cemetery with the priest. There was something familiar about the guy, so I stopped the car and got out. I walked over to the two of them. As soon as I saw his face, I knew who it was." Ignazzio told Trish about his tearful reunion with Nicolo.

"So what does that have to do with me?"

"Nicolo told me about you. He said you were a good friend."

"So?"

"Let me explain. A few weeks after I saw him, my neighbor mentioned there was a burial at the church. Usually, they announce it when somebody dies, but I didn't hear nothing, so I went over and seen some guys digging right by Nicolo's family's graves. I asked what funeral home they were with, and they said they were from New Jersey."

Trish wondered if all Sicilians told stories this way, expressing every little detail. That's how Mr. C talked, and it strained her short attention span.

"They were digging next to the Catania family, so I bent to look at the sign they stuck in the dirt. I almost fell over when I saw Nicolo Catania's name. I couldn't believe it. I just talked to him a few weeks ago, and now he's dead. I gotta tell you, when Nicolo mentioned he had a good friend named Patricia, I thought it was a girlfriend. A couple of times when I drove down to Jersey to look for you, that's what I thought, but unless you like old guys, I figure you was just a friend." He laughed.

"Yeah, well, I'm sorry for your loss, Mr. Guarino. I gotta go now."

"Wait, please. Nicolo told me about the money he wanted you to have. I can help you find it."

Recently shaken in her ability to read people, Trish wasn't sure if she should trust this guy. Why wouldn't Mr. C have mentioned an old friend?

"I don't know what you're talking about, Mr. Guarino. I think you got the wrong person, or you didn't understand him. I don't know anything about any money."

"Please think about what I said, Patricia. I can help you."

"Nice talking to you. Bye."

Trish's hand shook so hard she had trouble putting the phone back in its wall cradle. A chill invaded her entire body. She felt as if she were standing naked on an iceberg. She wished Gabby was home.

IT WAS NEARLY midnight when Gabby let herself into the apartment. She tiptoed into the bedroom and observed Trish, who seemed to be asleep. Gabby undressed and slipped into bed maneuvering to rest her cold feet against the backs of Trish's legs.

"What did you do that for?" Trish growled.

"I wanted to see if you were really sleeping."

"Well, not now."

"Trish, I can't stand this not talking. If you're still mad at me, yell or scream or say something. Not talking won't solve anything. What do you want me to do, kill myself?"

Oh boy, here comes big drama, Trish thought. "I'm listening if you want to talk."

"I've been thinking about this every minute since I left for San Juan, and I think I figured out what the problem is."

"The problem is you lied to me for no good reason."

"Yeah, I lied, but the question is why. I'm not making excuses for what I did. It was wrong, and I'm sorry. But there's more to it." Gabby raised herself up on one elbow. "You hate your parents and have nothing to do with your brother and sisters. It's not your fault. If my parents were like yours, I'd probably have no contact with them either. It's awful what they did to you, but from what you tell me, they weren't good parents even before they tossed you out."

Trish listened and threw up her guard. Gabby could be so persuasive that often Trish ended up giving in. This time, she was determined not to let her off the hook.

"Then you have me and my family. The reason I left Puerto Rico was to try to make a better life here. I've done okay, and I try to help them out a little. I tried to convince them to move here, but they're too set in their ways. They worry they won't be able to learn English, and my father thinks nobody will hire him. We talked about it when I was home last week, but they won't budge."

Trish interjected, "Don't forget about you not wanting them to know you're queer. Coming here was a good way to avoid dealing with that. You'd be living like a nun if you stayed there."

"I had a girlfriend there, but it wasn't easy. I admit it. I'm still close to my family, especially my sister. Not seeing them for years at a time hurts. You don't understand, or you don't want to."

"So this is my fault because I don't have a close family? That's why you lied about going to see yours? Pardon me, but my bullshit alarm is so loud it's making my head hurt."

"I didn't say it was your fault. You can't help it if family doesn't mean much to you. It's the way you grew up."

"Well, let me tell you something. Family is very important to me, maybe because I can't see mine. You're my family now, and when I found out I couldn't trust you, it was more painful than when my old man threw me out."

Gabby said through tears, "You know, we wouldn't be having this problem if it wasn't for that goddamned money. The minute you brought that bag of money into the apartment I had a bad feeling. See what it's doing? It's filthy money. Let's give it away."

Trish turned and pulled Gabby close as she sobbed out the pain of the last couple of weeks. She buried her head in Gabby's curls while she stroked her back.

"It's okay, Gabby. We'll get through this. Let's not fight anymore."

Gabby turned so they could assume their favorite spoons

position, and they fell asleep.

WHEN TRISH AWAKENED in the morning, she looked at Gabby's head still on the pillow they'd shared, and smiled. After days of unresolved anger, she felt relief knowing that as much as Gabby missed her San Juan family, she missed Trish more. She kissed Gabby's cheek before getting out of bed.

A short while later, Gabby sipped her steaming coffee while Trish prepared toast the way Gabby liked it, lightly browned with a quarter inch of butter on one half and grape jelly on the other. She pushed the plate across to Gabby and welcomed an approving smile. While Gabby ate, Trish told her about Ignazzio Guarino's call. The furrow between Gabby's eyebrows deepened as she listened.

"I don't know about this guy, Trish. You say he sounds legit, but so do all con men."

Trish removed Mr. C's letter from her bathrobe pocket and reread it. "Honestly, I don't know how we'd ever find anything with this map. And another thing, what's so important about this cemetery that Ignazzio just happened to be watching it when Mr. C was there?"

"You just said it. If Mr. C actually told him about the money, or if this guy was one of the bank robbers, he'd keep an eye on the cemetery to see if anybody strange was lurking around. If we went there and tried to find the money, I bet he'd be watching us. He might want us to lead him to the money, and once we found it..." Gabby made a slicing motion across her throat.

Trish winced. "You really think so? Put on your detective hat, Gabby. Can you think of any other reasons this guy might be trying to connect with me?"

"Maybe Mr. C did help rob the bank and then ripped those men off. If he took their share of the money, and didn't tell them where he put it, this Ignazzio might have been waiting all these years to see who tries to find it."

"Yeah, if that was true, the whole story he told me about being an old friend of Mr. C's was a lie. I'm sure Mr. C wouldn't have had dinner with one of those bank robbers for old time's sake, though."

"I can't think of any other reasons," Gabby said. "How are

you gonna decide?"

"I have no clue. Maybe I'll flip a coin."

"You still want to go to Gloversville?"

"Part of me wants to go, and another part says not to. One thing I'd like to know is if Mr. C might have any living relatives. If his brothers had kids, they should get his money. I wonder if Ignazzio knew Mr. C's brothers. He should if he was a friend of the family. Let's make a list of things we want to know. Next time he calls, if he calls, I'll ask him."

Trish got a sheet of paper and wrote, 'Iggy's Questions.'

"Oh, so now he's Iggy?" Gabby laughed. "Put down the question about any relatives. No, wait. First ask if he knew the brothers. Let's see. Oh, yeah, ask him when Mr. C's parents died and the brothers, too. We want to know if they all died at the same time. If they did, they might have been murdered cause Mr. C didn't help rob the bank. And while you're at it, ask him if he knows why Mr. C left Gloversville. Mr. C must have told him something if they really were old friends."

Trish wrote quickly. "I thought of another question. How about if I ask him if he knows how Mr. C got all this money?"

"I don't know, Trish. If you ask him about the money, he might be afraid you'll call the cops if it was from a bank robbery. It would be interesting to see what he says, though. He might hang up on you this time."

"The list is here by the phone. If you think of anything else, write it down."

For the next few days the phone was silent. By the end of the week, Trish's nightly leg cramps had eased. When she thought of Ignazzio, she heard the gentle voice with an Italian accent. Too bad he sounds so nice, she mused.

Chapter Eight

"I'VE MADE A decision," Trish announced when Gabby got home.

"Great. I'm starving. I was going to make a peanut butter and jelly sandwich."

"Huh? What are you talking about?"

"Supper. What are you cooking?"

Trish laughed. "Okay, let's start this conversation over. I'm not talking about food. I meant I decided we should meet Ignazzio in Gloversville."

Gabby waited before responding. "You sure about this?"

"Of course not. I'm nervous as hell. I want you to come with me."

"Is it time to knock off good old Uncle Paddy?"

"Yeah, for the girls at work, at least."

IGNAZZIO CALLED THE following week and Trish grabbed the list of questions. According to his recollections, he told Trish Mr. C's parents died within a week of each other. His father had a heart attack and, a few days after the funeral, his mother had a massive stroke. She died a few days later. To Trish, it sounded like both died of natural causes, which could have meant Mr. C did help rob the bank with the brothers from Sicily. Even the death of his brothers supported that theory. One brother fell off a ladder outside his house, hit his head on the pavement, and never recovered. The other one drowned when his fishing boat capsized on a nearby lake. That brother, his oldest, was in his seventies, so he lived a long time after the bank robbery. Trish searched for reasons to convince herself and Gabby that Mr. C didn't participate in the robbery, but wasn't coming up with anything satisfactory.

Gabby's reaction to the information wasn't what Trish expected. "It doesn't sound good for Mr. C, but it's still not proof he was a bank robber."

"When I asked Ignazzio if he had any idea how Mr. C got so much money, he said, 'Sometimes it's better if you don't know things.' That doesn't sound good to me."

"Did you ask him why Mr. C left Gloversville?"

"Oh yeah, this was the best part. He said it had something to do with a woman. He danced around it a little. Said something about Nicolo not being ready to have a family. Sounds to me like he knocked some girl up and didn't want to marry her. Maybe she had a botched abortion and died. That would have been enough to make him leave town if her family was after him."

"I don't know, Trish. I think if Mr. C had a kid, he would have at least sent money to the girl."

"Yeah, if she had the baby."

Trish shook her head. "I can't believe he would have been so cold. This doesn't sound like the sweet old man I knew."

Trish held up two fingers and immediately wished she hadn't.

"What's that mean? Gabby asked.

"Remember the vendetta Mr. C mentioned in his letter?"

"Yeah, you said he got beat up and did something to the kid."

"You better sit down. There's more to it that I didn't tell you."

Gabby pulled two chairs out from the dinette table and motioned for Trish to sit with her.

"When Mr. C was a kid, he played the violin. Apparently, he was good enough at it that his grandfather arranged for him to study with some famous teacher, so he could play concerts and stuff. Before he could go live with the teacher and study, a bunch of punks beat him up and broke his arm real bad. Even after a couple of surgeries, he couldn't feel anything in these two fingers." She held up the forefinger and middle finger of her left hand.

"Jesus, Maria y Jose. So he couldn't play the violin after that?" Tears formed and teetered on the edge of Gabby's eyelids.

"Right. He showed me an ugly scar that ran from his wrist halfway up his arm. That's why he wore long sleeves all the time.

"That's so disgusting. Don't tell me any more." Gabby got up and walked into the other room.

Trish followed her and asked, "So, are you going to come

with me? Ignazzio says he'll try to figure out where the money is.
I said I thought it might be in the cemetery. He says he knows
where every Italian in town is buried, which is more than we
know."

"Did he say if there are any living relatives?"

"He says neither brother had kids because they had mumps. I
didn't know what he meant."

"Mumps makes guys sterile." Gabby laughed and explained,
"When I was in high school, the boys told their girlfriends they
had mumps so the girls would think they couldn't get pregnant.
We knew they were full of it, though."

"I even asked Ignazzio if the brothers' wives were alive.
Nope. They're dead, too."

"So, if we find the money, there's nobody who should get it,
right? We still don't know if it's hot money. If the cop in that
newspaper story was right about the bills being unmarked, we
have to decide if we'll turn it over to the cops or...maybe give
most of it away."

"Most of it? Do I hear you changing your mind? I'm not interested in giving the money to the cops. I say we try to find the
money and then decide what to do. Are you with me?"

"There's no way I'm letting you go up there by yourself. If
they're gonna shoot you, they might as well shoot me, too. I don't
want to live without you."

"I know, babe. Me neither."

TRISH AND GABBY spent the next couple of weeks dropping
hints at work about poor old Uncle Paddy.

"I feel like we're playing God," Gabby said, over supper one
night "It's hard coming up with a new symptom of cancer every
few days."

Trish firmed up arrangements with Ignazzio and promised to
call him when they knew what time they'd arrive in Gloversville.
He gave her the name of a motel and said he'd pick them up at
the bus station. The trip began to sound more like an interesting
adventure and less scary. Even Gabby admitted that he sounded
okay.

"Let's make sure we've got our story straight for the girls.
The hospital called last night and said your uncle's kidneys are

failing, and it can't be more than a couple of days before he dies. So, we're leaving tomorrow to go up to Saugerties to see him. Have I got it right?"

"Perfect, and you're going with me to help with funeral arrangements. Remember, he's my father's brother, and my father is too sick to go himself. None of the other kids can do it, and I'm Uncle Paddy's favorite."

"Right. Got it." Gabby left for work.

Trish wasn't due at work until eleven, so she packed and thought about how all of this might play out. Gabby said they didn't need to quit until they decided about the money. She also thought two weeks' notice was plenty.

Getting to the diner five minutes early, Trish found her boss in his office. She walked in and closed the door.

"What's up?" he asked, and pushed aside the giant black checkbook he used to pay bills.

Trish began the spiel she'd practiced on the bus. "My only uncle has cancer, and the hospital says if I want to say goodbye to him, I better get there no later than tomorrow. It's in New York State. I'm sorry it's short notice, but if I don't go tomorrow, he could be dead."

"Sure, don't worry about it. I'll get the girls to cover. You know family comes first with me. You going by train?"

"No, bus is cheaper. Listen...Gabby's offered to go with me to help out with the funeral and stuff. My uncle's alone, no wife or kids, so I have to take care of everything. I never did this before."

He agreed grudgingly then began calculating. "Let's see. You need at least one day for the wake and then the funeral...if he dies day after tomorrow..."

Trish grew irritated about the way he did the math like he was ordering a side of beef. For the moment, she forgot the whole story was a lie.

"No family but me, so there won't be a wake. He's not religious, so I'm not sure there will be a mass. He wants to be cremated."

"He's not Catholic? I thought your family was."

"Yeah, he is, but he hasn't been in a church since he had a fight with the priest about forty years ago."

"You'd be surprised how many people still want last rites at the end. They want to make sure they don't go to Hell."

Trish and Gabby headed for the door when Rosalie approached them. "Here," she said, and pushed a thick envelope at Trish. "You'll need this, and the girls want you to have it." Rosalie sent them off with hugs.

"Boy, if I didn't already feel guilty about lying to our friends, this makes me feel like a real shit," Trish said, and showed Gabby the envelope Rosalie had given her.

"We'll give it back to them before we quit," Gabby said.

TRISH FOUND IT impossible to sleep that night and even Gabby, who usually slept through everything, tossed and turned. Gabby would nap on the bus, but Trish worried that she'd arrive in Gloversville feeling like a zombie. She gave up at a few minutes past five and went into the kitchen to make coffee. While it percolated, Gabby appeared in the kitchen doorway wearing Trish's bathrobe.

"You couldn't sleep, either?"

"I heard you turn off the alarm, and I couldn't go back to sleep. Figured I might as well shower."

"Want coffee now or after?"

"Now...no after. I need to get into a hot shower. My neck is stiff. Must've slept funny."

"Tension," Trish said.

"Better a stiff neck than hives, I guess."

"Wait a minute, babe. Turn around."

"What? Did I do something wrong?"

"No, you look so cute in my robe. It could go around you twice. Too bad it only comes to your knees."

"Is this better?" Gabby undid the belt and dropped the robe to the floor in one swift movement.

"Hmm, I'll say it is." Trish closed the distance between them and took Gabby in her arms.

She was shocked when Gabby pushed her away.

"I haven't even brushed my teeth yet. You know I don't like doing it in the morning. Sorry, babe. We'll have plenty of time to make love in the motel. We can screw our brains out like we did in Cape May. Isn't that what motels are for?" As she bent to retrieve the robe, Trish admired the view.

"Yeah, they say it keeps the roaches away. Go shower your neck. If you want, I can put Ben Gay on it when you come out."

THE BUS CAREENED around several corners after exiting the New York Thruway and finally slowed down, easing into a space at the side of the Gloversville bus station that doubled as a hardware store.

"Wake up, babe," Trish said, and nudged Gabby's arm. "Look how pretty the snow is. It started about half an hour ago."

Trish slung the plastic tote bag containing boots over her shoulder and they got off the bus. While waiting for the driver to get their suitcase out of the baggage compartment, she looked around and spotted a good-looking older guy with dark curly hair standing about twenty feet away. His hands were in his jacket pockets, and he was shifting from one foot to the other. He wore earmuffs and a scarf, but his cheeks were red and tears dripped from his dark eyes. Most people in the parking lot wore heavy coats or parkas, but he had on a lightweight leather jacket. Trish waved and he walked toward them and smiled. The bus driver swung their suitcase onto the sidewalk.

"You're Patricia, right?" he said, as he reached for the suitcase. "I'm Ignazzio."

"This is Gabby."

"We've sort of met before," he said, with a broad grin. "I hope you don't still want to shoot me."

Gabby looked down as she replied, "Not while you're carrying our suitcase."

"My car's right over here. Follow me."

Trish and Gabby got into the back seat of a shiny black Buick. Not bad, Trish thought. She wondered if he was in the same line of work Mr. C might have been in.

"You're staying at the Clover Leaf Motel, right?"

"Yeah. You said it was the best place in town."

"Well, it's the only place. I hope it's okay."

Trish studied Ignazzio as he drove and realized he was older than Esther had described. His hair was more salt than pepper, and she guessed he was probably around sixty-five, which would have made him younger than Mr. C. With his scarf loosened, his muscular neck reminded her of some football players she sat behind in school.

Ignazzio insisted on carrying their suitcase into the motel office and seemed to know the woman at the desk.

"Must be a town where everybody knows everyone," Gabby whispered.

Once they registered, he carried the suitcase to their room and watched while Trish unlocked the door. He put it on a luggage stand.

"There's a pizza joint next door or, if you don't want pizza, there's a Chinese place a couple of blocks from here. Are you hungry? I could drive you if you want."

Gabby stood behind Ignazzio and mouthed the words *I have to pee*, so Trish thanked him and said they needed to get settled.

"Here's my number," he said, and handed Trish a piece of paper. "It's local, so give me a call in the morning and we can have a cup of coffee and figure out what to do." Looking at the sneakers on Gabby's feet, he advised, "We're not supposed to get more than an inch or two of snow, but you might want to wear boots if you brought them."

Gabby did a quick inspection of the bathroom and reported, "It's clean, but a little shabby. Some of the paint over the shower is peeling. The person who put in the floor tiles must have had one too many. Don't look at the floor or you might get dizzy. The shower is clean and the toilet looks newer than the rest of the stuff." Moving to the bureau she asked, "Think it's okay to put our underwear in the dresser?"

"The place looks fine, but if you're worried about it, keep it in the suitcase."

"I'm starving. Let's go eat," Gabby said.

The short walk to the Chinese restaurant was enough to put Trish into a deep freeze. Even wearing her warmest mittens, it took ten minutes for her hands to thaw after they sat down in a booth. She wrapped her hands around a small teacup and, even though she really didn't like tea, she refilled her cup often so she could warm her fingers.

Trish took Mr. C's letter out and read it while they waited for their food. She hoped Ignazzio could make sense out of what was in it. The line about keeping close to the Holy Spirit still baffled both women. Could Mr. C have meant it as a joke?

Gabby's good night kiss was the last thing Trish remembered

before waking up shortly after five with her teeth chattering. She noted Gabby's jacket draped over her blanket and slipped into the bed beside her. She wrapped herself around her lover, making as much body contact as possible. Gabby moaned acknowledgment and resumed snoring. Trish warmed up a bit, but never did get back into a deep sleep.

As the room lightened, Trish saw frost on the inside of the window where the faded drapes didn't quite close and rejected any thought of living farther north than Newark. Her fantasy of living in Maine ended abruptly at the sight of that frosted window.

"Time to get up," Trish said, and rubbed Gabby's neck. She went into the bathroom and created a cloud of steam.

"Bring my clothes in here, please. I can't bear the thought of coming out there and having icicles hang off my tits."

Gabby skipped a shower, dressed, and went to the lobby in search of hot coffee. By the time she returned with two cups, she heard a tapping sound coming from the wall heater. "Thank God. They must turn the heat off after a certain time. Maybe we can offer to add five bucks to our bill if they'll leave the heat on tonight. I can't stand being cold."

"Better get used to it if we're going to be in the cemetery looking for the grave Mr. C told us about," Trish warned.

"I hate cemeteries, Trish. Maybe I can wait in the car."

"What are you afraid of? It's broad daylight. Ghouls don't come out till dark. I'll protect you."

Gabby glanced over at Trish and smiled. "We wouldn't have to freeze our asses off in Puerto Rico."

Trish sneered and dialed Ignazzio's number. "Hmm, I'm surprised he's not answering. He was so gung-ho to help us find the money."

The women bundled up in every piece of warm clothing they'd brought and walked down the sidewalk to the office.

Chapter Nine

"GOOD MORNING, LADIES," a man's voice called from behind a large ginger jar lamp in the lobby.

"Ignazzio, I just called you," Trish said.

"I figured you'd be up by now, so I drove over. Are you ready for breakfast?"

"Something hot and delicious would be fine with me."

"There's a great diner not far from here. You like diners?"

Trish and Gabby laughed. "We work in one," they said in unison.

Ignazzio led the way to his idling car. They welcomed the warm blast of air as he opened the door.

"Boy, you can tell we're not in Newark anymore," Trish remarked. "If you left your keys in a running car, it would have disappeared in five minutes."

"It's one of the nice things about living in a small town. Everybody knows everybody and, except for an occasional tourist from down state, people don't steal from each other."

Gabby asked, "Don't you ever get tired of everybody knowing your business? I think that would get on my nerves."

"We call it looking out for each other around here. It's nice when people offer to help out if you need it."

Trish thought something was odd about Ignazzio's speech but let it go.

Vinny's Diner had the best French toast Trish had ever eaten. The challah bread soaked up the batter like a sponge and took on a golden hue. Unlike Scotty's, this diner served real maple syrup. After licking it off her fork and fingers, Trish decided she'd never again be happy with Log Cabin syrup.

Gabby tried the creamed chipped beef. Despite her comment about it resembling wallpaper paste, she cleaned her plate.

Trish asked, "So, Ignazzio, what do you do when you're not helping strangers?"

"I'm in construction. Right now, there's not much work, so I kick back and relax."

I'm in the wrong line of work, Gabby reflected as she thought of his shiny new Buick.

After the waitress cleared the dirty dishes, Trish took out Mr. C's letter. Before she could share the contents, Gabby asked, "So, you were a friend of Nicolo's family?"

"Yeah, they were great people. They sort of adopted me, since I had no other family here."

"Did you know the girl Nicolo got pregnant?"

"I...uh...no, she didn't live in Gloversville. Nicolo must have met her when he traveled for work."

"But Nicolo worked in the post office," Trish said.

"He...uh...had lots of jobs. Always hustling to make a buck."

Trish opened the letter. "Do you know anybody around here named Tredita?"

"If the name ends in a vowel, I probably do. Why?"

"Mr. C, I mean Nicolo, said we should find a grave with that name."

While Trish and Gabby put on their coats and scarves, Ignazzio slid a tip beneath his saucer and went to the register to pay the check. After he left the table, Trish checked to be sure he did right by the waitress.

"Well, let's go to the cemetery and start looking. Did he tell you which cemetery?"

"There's more than one?" Trish asked.

"We got three in town, but I think we should start with the one where Nicolo and his family are buried. Okay with you?"

They got back into Ignazzio's car, which by then was cold and smelled like a wet dog. He drove slowly on the glazed streets, parting a light curtain of snowflakes. In fewer than five minutes, they reached the Church of the Holy Spirit.

They followed Ignazzio into the gray stone church and Gabby and Trish looked at each other as he crossed himself with holy water. Trish thought it odd that he didn't genuflect at the head of the main aisle opposite the altar. Gabby suppressed a smile as she gazed at the vaulted roof, and Trish placed a protective hand on the top of her head.

"Father Rocco is the priest here," Ignazzio explained. "He knows where every grave is located. He probably baptized and confirmed almost every Catholic in town. Buried lots of them, too."

Trish sensed sadness in this church, a very different feeling from Sacred Heart Cathedral where she went as a kid. Stale incense hung in the air from a recent mass, and the church was empty except for a little old priest who seemed to be expecting them. He toddled up the aisle, his brown robes rustling as they brushed the worn wooden pews.

"Welcome to Holy Spirit," he said.

"Father, meet Patricia and Gabby from New Jersey. Ladies, this is Father Rocco Bellarugosa." The priest shook their hands. "They were friends of Nicolo Catania, and they want to see his grave."

"Ah yes, Nicolo. I didn't see him for many years, but I remember when his family moved to Gloversville. Nice people. Very nice. I'm sorry about Nicolo. The undertaker said he didn't want a mass or funeral, but I prayed for him anyway while they put the coffin in. He's home with our Father now, so you should not be sad."

Sad? The priest sure didn't know Mr. C very well. Trish was surprised he didn't jump out of the coffin to tell the priest not to pray for him. Not likely he's with Jesus, she thought. At least, she hoped he wasn't burning in Hell.

"Why don't you show them his grave? I'll wait here." Ignazzio rubbed his hands together and blew on them. Trish wondered why he wouldn't have gotten used to the cold living in Gloversville all those years.

Father Rocco led them out the heavy iron-framed side door and up the uneven worn stone path to the cemetery. "Stay close to the Holy Spirit," Mr. C's letter said. Trish was certain the money must be there. Partway up the path, Father Rocco stopped.

"If you want, I can hear your confessions."

Trying to head off a possible wisecrack from Gabby, Trish jumped in. "No, thank you, Father."

"In case you change your mind, I'm here all day, every day."

Trish was unsure of cemetery etiquette. She wasn't aware of any requirement to confess before visiting a grave. She looked back at Gabby and shrugged her shoulders.

Father Rocco led the way past old and sometimes crumbling grave markers. Just like in life, Trish thought, as they passed some well-maintained huge ornamental tombstones and other small ones with chipped and faded chiseled letters. Poor people can't even get a fair shake in death.

Trish slid on the slick snow and reached for Gabby's arm. The priest seemed to know every inch of the terrain and, surprisingly for a man his age, inched along like a sure-footed goat, oblivious to the sucking sound of his open-topped galoshes.

Finally, he stopped and pointed to a snow-covered mound of dirt with a temporary sign covered in plastic. "Here is your friend. It's too cold to place the stone, but I can tell you where the shop is if you want to see it. They'll put it up in the spring."

"Are you sure this is Nicolo's grave?" Trish asked.

"Oh yes. I saw them lower his coffin into it." He indicated the stick with the small hand-lettered sign bearing the name, Nicolo Catania. Then pointing a few feet away he said, "There are his parents' graves and also his brothers'. Take your time. I'll wait for you in the church." He retraced his steps, and they watched as he struggled for a few seconds with the weight of the heavy door.

For a moment, they stood quietly. The flat midday light cast a pall over the tombstones. The sun shone briefly but within seconds the clouds had pushed it away, allowing more snow to fall on this sad place.

Never at a loss for words, Gabby said, "Thanks for dying so close to winter, Mr. C. You could have picked better weather."

"Gabby, have a little respect."

"What are we supposed to do now? Do you think he knows we're here?"

"I don't know, but I'm gonna talk to him just in case. Well, Mr. C," Trish began, "we made it this far. So give us a clue. Where is the money? If you can hear us, tell us where Tredita is."

At that moment, a clump of snow fell from an overhanging branch. Gabby jumped and grabbed Trish's arm. "Holy shit, Trish. Maybe it's a sign."

Trish smacked Gabby's arm. "Stop it. Be serious." She walked over to the graves of Mr. C's parents, Concetta and Luigi Catania. The engraved dates in the still partially glossy, gray granite told her Mr. C's mother was a year older than his father. Also, Ignazzio was right. She died a week and five days after her husband. Wandering farther, she saw the graves of his brothers and their wives.

Some of the older graves had framed photos of the deceased attached to the stones. Maybe Mr. C had put money behind a photo on Tredita's tombstone. That sure would be preferable to imagine than other possible scenarios.

Trish said, "I feel like one of those creeps who pokes around in the medicine chest when they use your bathroom." She moved away from the family plots, searching for the name Tredita. "I wonder if the church keeps a map of where people are buried."

"I think we're on a wild goose chase," Gabby said. "How're we gonna check out all the graves without Father Rocco getting suspicious?"

"Maybe we'll have to come back at night after he's asleep."

"Whoa, babe. Count me out. I'm not roaming around a cemetery in the dark. It's spooky enough in the daytime. Besides, if you think it's cold now, it'll be twenty or thirty degrees colder at night." She playfully grabbed at Trish's chest. "You'll freeze these right off."

"Yeah, dumb idea. Let's see what Ignazzio thinks."

They threaded their way carefully between rows of graves and back through the gate.

When they entered the church, they heard Ignazzio say to somebody as he closed a door, "I'll call you later."

He walked briskly toward them. "Did you see Nicolo's grave?"

"We saw a mound of dirt that Father Rocco says is Nicolo's grave. There's no tombstone on it, but he says he saw them put the coffin in it. Do you think there's a diagram of where the graves are that lists the names?"

Ignazzio pulled a piece of paper out of his pocket. "Great minds think alike, ladies. I asked Father Rocco for a copy. Let's sit over here and take a look." They followed him to a weathered pew in the middle of the church. Sitting between them, he opened the paper and spread it over his knees. "What was the name you said Nicolo told you to look for?"

"Tredita."

The copy was very dark, and Trish squinted in the dim light. "Let's move closer to the light."

Their jackets scraped along the wooden pew as they inched toward the edge. Briefly, Trish wondered if Mr. C had ever sat there.

They scanned all of the names and didn't find any Tredita. "It must be here," Trish insisted. "He said I should stay close to the

Holy Spirit, and that's the name of this church. Is there another cemetery named Holy Spirit?"

"Maybe he meant you should go to church or keep the faith," Ignazzio said.

As if on cue, Father Rocco appeared and approached them. He gestured toward the confessional. "If you want me to hear your confessions, there's no line."

Trish exhaled loudly and shook her head. "Father, you ever hear of a family named Tredita?"

He attempted to hold up three arthritic fingers.

"You a Boy Scout?" Ignazzio asked.

"Tredita means three fingers. No, I never knew a family by that name."

"Oh...right. Yeah, three fingers."

Gabby drew her jacket tighter and pushed her hands into her pockets.

Ignazzio said, "Come on, let's go someplace and get hot coffee."

THE CAR NEVER warmed up by the time they reached the diner, so Trish and Gabby pulled their wool hats down over their ears and sprinted to the door. They darted inside and found a booth far from the door. Within a few minutes, Ignazzio joined them. Soon, the women loosened their scarves and removed their jackets. The diner felt like the tropics, making it impossible to see out the steamy windows.

Noticing beads of sweat on Ignazzio's forehead, Gabby suggested, "Why don't you take your jacket off?"

"Nah, I'm fine. It's the hot coffee. Always makes me sweat." He wiped the droplets off with a napkin.

"So, what now? No Tredita in the cemetery. Are we at a dead end?" Gabby poked Trish and they shared a laugh.

Ignazzio's blank look prompted Trish to say, "Dead end? Cemetery? Get it?"

"There are two other Catholic cemeteries near here. We could check them. I don't know the priests over there, though, so I'm not sure we could get a diagram. We might have to walk around and check the stones."

"Ugh. Maybe we should come back and do this in the

spring," Gabby said.

"If you're too cold, I could go and check them out and let you know what I find. You came all this way. It would be a shame not to at least see if we can find it."

"Even if we find the grave, what are we gonna do?" Trish asked. "We can't dig it up. Maybe the money is in a coffin with a body."

Gabby nodded. "Too bad we didn't think this through before we left Newark. The more I think about it, the dumber this whole thing sounds."

"Why don't I take you back to the motel? I'll go check on those other cemeteries. It shouldn't take more than a few hours. I'll come get you later and we can grab supper. I know a nice little Italian restaurant right outside Gloversville. We can fill our stomachs and figure out what to do. Don't get discouraged. We'll figure something out."

Trish sighed. "Okay. At least we should eat some good food so the day isn't a total loss."

BACK AT THE motel office, Trish asked, "Is there any way you could leave the heat on tonight? We froze last night."

"Since you're the only ones staying tonight, I don't want to heat the whole place, but I have a space heater you can use. Just don't put it near the curtains or bedding." She returned to the desk and Trish gratefully accepted the heater.

"Let's try it out," Gabby urged, as soon as they returned to their room. She plugged it in and in a few minutes unclenched her hands. "Did you double lock the door?"

"Yeah, and I'm gonna put the chair in front like I saw in a movie in case somebody tries to get in." She dragged the faded brown plaid club chair in front of the door. "I meant to do this last night."

Gabby removed her jacket and boots and squirmed out of her sweater. Trish watched and smiled in a way that could mean only one thing. "You getting ready to take a nap?" she teased.

"Come over here and find out."

Two hours later, Trish opened her eyes and looked around. It took a few seconds before it registered that she was in the motel. "Jesus, it's hot in here," she said. "What'd you set the heater on?

It must be eighty degrees in here."

Gabby, awakening from twilight sleep, replied, "It's not the heater, hot stuff. It's you. I gotta take you to motels more often."

Trish sniffed deeply. "Don't know about you, but I need a shower. Be sure not to let Ignazzio in here. This place smells like the back seat of a car that just came from a drive-in."

"You think he'd have a problem with us? Mr. C knew, and he didn't."

"Well, that was different. We were his only friends. Besides, as far as I knew, he never married. Who knows? Until Ignazzio told us about him getting that girl pregnant, I thought maybe he was one of us."

"Getting somebody pregnant doesn't mean anything. We know lots of people who married for convenience."

With not a minute to spare, both women showered and dressed. Trish reached for the ringing phone.

"You have a visitor," the desk clerk announced.

"Is he tall, dark, and handsome?"

"Not bad," the woman replied, laughing.

Chapter Ten

"UMM, THIS CALAMARI is to die for." Trish dipped another ring of the lightly breaded squid into marinara sauce.

"Glad you like it. I think this is the best Italian food around here, and that's saying something. Wait till you taste the rest. I ordered three dishes so you can sample a variety. I didn't know if you were familiar with Italian food."

Trish said, "When I was younger, I lived for a while with my friend Angela's family. Boy, could her mother cook. I must have gained three pounds a week while I lived there."

Three entrees turned out to be large enough for several people. After inhaling the aroma of eggplant parmigiana, beef braciole and shrimp scampi, plus a huge bowl of fettucine with meat sauce, they tried valiantly to do it justice. Ignazzio ended up taking nearly half of the food home.

"I hope you saved room for dessert," Ignazzio said, as the waitress delivered huge servings of homemade tiramisu soaked in rum and creamy panna cotta.

"Even if we don't find the money," Gabby said, as she savored the sweet creamy perfection, "This makes the trip worth it. My God, this must be what they serve in Heaven."

Trish discreetly reached under her sweater, undid the top button of her slacks, and asked, "So, what did you find at the other cemeteries?"

Ignazzio wiped his mouth and shook his finger. "No business until we finish eating. It's bad for digestion."

Over hot cups of cappuccino they enjoyed popular music by Sinatra, Dean Martin, and Vic Damone. Each time the last record dropped, the waitress restacked them and started all over.

The restaurant windows steamed up from the hot food, and the effect was like looking out through a frosty beer mug at the lights of the passing cars. The small dining room was decorated with strands of colored lights and tinsel, giving it a Christmassy look even though it was only the first week in December. It reminded Trish of the feasts she'd attended at various neighborhood Italian churches. She could almost smell the frying calzones and taste the sausage and peppers all over again.

Ignazzio used his fork to scrape up the last few crumbs of tiramisu and pushed his plate away. "So, you wanna hear about my search of the graveyards? There's good news and bad news. Which do you wanna hear first?"

"You choose," Gabby replied.

"Okay, good news first. I got diagrams of both cemeteries. The bad news is I thought there were two other Catholic cemeteries, but it turns out one of them is Jewish, so that's not gonna help us. The Catholic one ran out of graves before the First World War, so Tredita's probably not buried there. I double-checked and the latest date I found was 1907."

"Shit," Trish muttered loud enough for Ignazzio and Gabby to hear, but hopefully nobody else.

"Pardon me for asking a dumb question," Gabby said, "but do all Italians have to be Catholic?" She looked to Ignazzio. "I remember kids in school joking about Columbus being Jewish. He was Italian, right?"

Raising his eyebrows, Ignazzio answered, "I don't think there's a law about it, but every Italian I ever met was Catholic. I can ask Father Rocco. He'd know."

"Ninety-five percent of the kids I went to school with were Italian, and I'm pretty sure they were all Catholic," Trish said. "On Ash Wednesday, every kid in the school, except for two Jews, got excused to come in late so they could get ashes. We used to tell the Jews they should put cigarette ashes on their heads so they could come in late, too."

"If I remember my history, Columbus was Spanish, not Italian, but he sailed from Genoa,Italy when he came to America. I love studying history. It helps make sense of this crazy world. It gives you perspective," Ignazzio bragged.

"Reason I asked is, if Jews could be Italian, Tredita could be in the Jewish cemetery. Maybe we should check there to be sure."

"I don't mind. We could go tomorrow. The weather's supposed to be warmer."

Trish glanced at Gabby's glassy eyes and stifled a yawn. "It's getting to be my bedtime," she said. "Are we ready to leave?"

Ignazzio paid the bill. "Give me a few minutes to warm up the car. I'll blink the lights when you should come out."

"I don't know what's come over me," Gabby said, as Trish held her jacket. "I feel like I could sleep right here."

Trish laughed at Gabby's inability to hold her wine. "And we had a nap this afternoon, too."

Gabby slipped her arms into her jacket and Trish turned expecting her to return the favor. She gave up after Gabby dropped her scarf and gloves on the floor. Gabby wobbled past a couple of tables and held onto the wall while Trish opened the door.

IT WAS A quiet ride back to the motel. Ignazzio pulled up to the door of their room and Trish agreed to call him in the morning. She steered Gabby across the pavement, and was surprised when a current of chilly air hit them as they entered the room.

"I could swear I left the heater on." Trish checked and sure enough, it had been unplugged.

"You did," Gabby answered. She flopped on her bed.

Since Gabby was as limp as a rag doll, Trish struggled to remove her boots. Getting the rest of her clothes off was a bit easier, but putting on her pajamas was more work than Trish wanted to tackle, so she tucked her in wearing only underpants and socks.

Trish sat on her bed and felt a draft. When she checked the window to be sure the drapes were closed, she saw a puddle of water on the sill. Seeing no moisture on the ceiling or adjacent walls, she didn't think it could be caused by condensation. Upon further inspection, she discovered the window was unlocked, and the top panel had slipped down about a quarter of an inch. She pushed it back up, turned the lock, and eased into bed. Within minutes, her muscles relaxed and she faded into sleep.

THE NEXT MORNING, Trish went to the office to fetch coffee while Gabby attempted to shower away her hangover.

Gabby dressed and slurped her coffee. Trish waited until the dark liquid reached the halfway point and Gabby's eyes looked functional. "What do you make of Ignazzio after spending some time with him?"

"I'd like to talk to him while he's wired to a lie detector. I

can't pinpoint anything, but I get the feeling he's full of it sometimes."

"I know what you mean. There've been a few times when I
wondered who this guy really is, but he always seems to have an
explanation." Suddenly, Trish shouted, "The accent! It comes and
goes. When I talked to him on the phone, he always had it, but
here he loses it sometimes."

"And something else," Gabby added. "For somebody who's
lived here as long as he says he has, you'd think he'd wear something warmer than an unlined leather jacket in this weather. I
don't know, babe. You think we're picking at stuff because we're
nervous? Maybe we need to cut him some slack. He seems nice
enough, and he didn't have to offer to help us."

"The guy was sweating bullets in the diner, but he wouldn't
take his jacket off," Trish said.

"He could have had a hole in his shirt," Gabby said.

"Oh, and last night saying Columbus was Spanish. Jesus
Christ. In Newark, the Sons of Italy own the Columbus Day
parade."

Gabby sighed. "What are we gonna do if we can't find Tredita's grave?"

"We go home and forget about it, but I keep thinking we're
missing something." She took out Mr. C's letter and scrutinized
it. "There's something we're not seeing. My mind is like a record
that's stuck in the groove. It repeats 'Keep close to the Holy
Spirit.' It's got to be in the cemetery of the church." She supported her head in her hands.

"Read it to me again," Gabby said.

Trish read the letter aloud.

"Read that last part again."

"Please remember me the way you knew me, and keep close
to the Holy Spirit."

"It sounds like a riddle. He didn't talk like that. Maybe we
should go back to the church without Ignazzio. If we read the letter while we're there, something might jump out at us."

"What are we gonna tell him? He'll think we don't want his
help."

"Tell him we want to spend time praying. I don't care what
you tell him, and I don't think he'll care either. It can't be fun for
him chauffeuring us around. Tell him he's off the hook for the

day, but we'll meet him for supper. Something about him gives me the creeps, anyway."

"A minute ago you wanted to cut him some slack. Make up your mind."

Before Trish could get Ignazzio's phone number out of her wallet, the phone rang. "Your friend is here," the desk clerk said, in a singsong way that hinted she was in on some romantic secret.

"Shit, he's here, babe. Now what?"

"If you don't want to tell him, I will."

"No, I'll do it. Lock the door after me."

As Trish walked slowly toward the office, she realized she was skipping cracks in the sidewalk the way she'd done on her way to school as a kid. Some old saw about stepping on a crack meant you'd break your grandmother's back.

"Good morning," she said. "Sit, please," she said, in response to Ignazzio rising to his feet. She sat next to him on the sofa.

"Am I too early? I could come back later."

"No, I came to tell you we're giving you the day off. You've been so nice, but we need some quiet time in the church to honor Mr. C's memory, I mean Nicolo. You know, praying for his soul and lighting candles. With no funeral, we never got a chance to do that. We'll grab a taxi in a while. I'm sure you have things to do."

"Nonsense. It's no trouble at all. I can drive you to the church and pick you up later. How much time do you think you need?"

"No, really, we'll be fine. You should go. We don't want to feel like we're on a schedule. Prayer takes a lot of time. I'm sure you understand. If you're free, we can call you and have supper together, if you want."

When Trish returned to their room, Gabby asked, "Well, did you get rid of our shadow?"

"Yeah, but he was persistent." She summarized the conversation with Ignazzio.

"I should have gone with you. I'd love to have seen you say it with a straight face."

Gabby cradled the phone book on her lap.

"What are you looking for?" Trish asked.

"I was curious, so I looked up Ignazzio in the local book. His name is Guarino, right? He's not in the book."

"So what? I'm not listed in our book, and neither are you.

Doesn't mean anything."

The sun peeked out while they waited in the lobby for a cab. "Maybe it'll melt this shit," Trish whispered, as they walked out in boots, scarves and hats, and with jackets buttoned to their chins. The sun felt good, but a biting wind tried to slip past their gloves and climb up their sleeves.

Chapter Eleven

TRISH AND GABBY weren't in the church five minutes when Father Rocco came out of his secret door, circled around behind the pews, and shuffled up the center aisle to where they sat.

"Good morning, ladies. Would you like me to hear your confessions?"

"Do we look like ax murderers?" Gabby blurted out.

He stood open-mouthed before replying, "I...I...don't understand. Excuse me."

Trish nudged Gabby.

"You keep wanting to hear our confessions like we did something awful. You got a quota you have to meet each month?"

"Shut up," Trish said, giving it her best ventriloquist effort.

"No, no, I just thought..." He walked away.

"Nice going. We might need his help, you know."

Gabby shrugged. "I guess I was a little over the top. Maybe I need some breakfast. Let's walk over to the diner. It's only a few blocks, and it's warmer than yesterday."

The sun glinted off the remaining light covering of snow. Gabby extended the brim of her hat with her hand. Trish wiped tears with a shredded tissue she dug out of her pocket.

Seated in a booth, Gabby said, "Don't look now, but Ignazzio is in the third booth on the other side of the door."

Trish twisted in time to see Ignazzio look out from behind his newspaper and wave with a grin.

"I'm going over to explain," Trish said. "I don't want him to think I lied."

"Hello again," she said, when she reached his booth. "We decided it would be better to pray on a full stomach. After last night's great dinner, I didn't think I'd want to eat again so soon, but the crisp air makes me hungry. We'll give you a call later. Enjoy your day."

"You shouldn't feel guilty about lying to him. Look at all the lies we've told our friends," Gabby urged, as Trish launched her butt at a space between two cracks in the plastic seat to avoid snagging her slacks. Gabby studied the menu and, when the waitress returned, they ordered.

Trish put her hot coffee cup next to a pat of butter and, when it softened, slathered it on a piece of toast. She made a silent promise not to eat the home fries that hugged the edges of the fried eggs, but scolded herself when she lost her resolve. No dessert tonight, she swore.

Relishing her blueberry pancakes, Gabby poured enough maple syrup on them to put everybody in the diner in a coma. Trish watched with envy, knowing her slim partner wouldn't gain an ounce.

BACK AT THE church, Gabby held the heavy wooden door for Trish and they scanned the church for signs of the priest. Too soon, he popped his head out. Trish assumed he had an alarm to tell him when somebody entered the church. Gabby's earlier remarks must have stung enough for him to retreat into his office. Trish walked around the pews gazing at the stained glass windows. She remembered many of the saints from her tortured hours in catechism classes. She smiled, recalling how two students shared a desk and stood, in turn, to spit back the memorized passages from the catechism when the prune-faced nun called on them.

The first saint she recognized was Anthony of Padua, the one who helped find lost things. Already developing into a smart ass, Trish asked the nun if the Virgin had lost Jesus because her calendar at home had a painting of Anthony handing the baby back to his mother. The nun smacked Trish's hand hard three times with a ruler, putting an end to her Catholic curiosity.

Trish continued perusing the stained glass windows. One window caught her eye, not for the memories it evoked, but for its beauty. "Come look at this, Gabby," she said softly, even though they were the only ones in the church. The window stood in a prominent place near the main altar and portrayed the Holy Spirit as a white dove. Trish recalled a Holy Spirit silver pendant she received when she made her first Holy Communion. Despite the religious significance, she'd always been partial to doves. On the window, the white dove spread its wings over a field of multi-hued gold rays. Behind the rays lay a beautiful royal blue background with yellow, white, and gold stars. She and Gabby stood together admiring the window and the way the sunlight filtered through it.

"This must be what heaven looks like," Trish said.

"Well, take a good look because you're never gonna see it unless Jesus comes off the cross and orders everybody to love queers."

"Can't you be serious for a minute? Don't you think it's beautiful?"

"I'd like it better if it was in a museum."

Trish scowled and halted her tour of the windows. "Let's go back to Mr. C's grave and see if anything registers about his letter."

The melting snow had left small puddles between the rows of graves. Several of the stones displayed carvings of the Holy Spirit, some so faded you could hardly see the outline of the dove. When they reached the Catania family's headstones, Trish noticed they were fairly plain, all except one which she presumed marked the grave of Mr. C's brother. Anthony Catania, who had died in 1948. He must have been the one who drowned, but something wasn't right. The engraving on his stone said 'Beloved son, brother, husband and father.' Ignazzio had told them neither of Mr. C's brothers had any kids. Maybe he was somebody else's brother, or perhaps his kids died. Trish wanted to ask Father Rocco who this guy was, but after Gabby smart-mouthed him, she was reluctant to bother him. She took a note pad and pen out of her purse and jotted his name down. Maybe Ignazzio could ask the priest. Trish and Gabby stood by Mr. C's grave hoping for inspiration.

Gabby said, "I wish I could ask him one last question. Where the hell is the money?"

DISGUSTED AT FINDING no clues in the church or the cemetery, Trish and Gabby dragged themselves back to the diner, their boots scraping along the partially dried sidewalk. They planned to call a taxi from a pay phone in the vestibule. Trish hated to admit that, yet again, Gabby had been right about this being a wild goose chase. She kicked herself for wasting time and money. When would she learn to trust Gabby's ESP?

They weren't more than ten steps from the diner when a car pulled alongside them and they heard a man's voice say, "Looking for a ride, girls?" Before Trish yielded to her New Jersey instinct to run, she realized it was Ignazzio.

Gabby walked around to the driver's side and leaned into the window. "We were gonna call a taxi, and here you are."

"At your service, ma'am. Where to?"

They got into the back seat and Gabby answered, "Newark, New Jersey, please."

Trish looked in the rearview mirror at Ignazzio's raised eyebrows. "You giving up?"

"Yeah, I'm starting to think Mr. C was playing one last joke on me," Trish explained. "He used to kid me all the time about going to church."

"I wish you'd give it more time. I've been thinking about what you said, Gabby, about Tredita maybe being Jewish. Let's check out the Jewish cemetery. You never can tell. We might get lucky."

"I've had it," Trish replied. "You go if you want. I'm ready for a nap." She stole a glance at Gabby, whose wink left no question about what she had in mind.

"Ignazzio made a wide U-turn and headed toward the motel. "When do you think you'll leave?"

"Tomorrow," Gabby and Trish replied in unison. "No point wasting another day here," Gabby added. "We need to get back to work."

As he pulled up in front of the motel, he asked, "Can we have dinner together tonight? If you're up for more Italian food, there's another good restaurant in town."

"Sounds good. Want to pick us up at six?"

"Your chariot will be here, ladies." Ignazzio jumped out of the car and rushed around to open the door, losing his footing in the slush. He went down on one knee and stopped himself from falling the rest of the way by grabbing the door handle. "Goddammit, what a klutz!" He brushed off his slacks and tried to laugh off his embarrassment.

"You okay?" Trish asked.

"Yeah, I'm fine. A little wet from the knee down. Good thing I didn't fall on my keister. At least nobody will think I wet myself."

After the women got out, Ignazzio went quickly to the driver's side, got in, and sped off.

"Wait!" Gabby called after his departing car as she stooped to pick up a worn leather wallet lying in the slush. "He's gonna croak when he discovers he dropped his wallet."

"You sure it's his? Maybe somebody else lost it."

They took the soggy wallet to their room and Trish opened it to be sure it was Ignazzio's before calling him. She found a Pennsylvania license for an Irwin Greenberg.

"Good thing I checked before I called. It's not Ignazzio's. It belongs to a guy named Greenberg from Philadelphia."

"We need to call him. Is there anything in there with a phone number? Maybe he's staying here. We can check at the desk."

Trish picked through a thin stack of photos and cards. "Holy shit, babe. Look at this." She pulled out an ID card for a Pinkerton agent named Greenberg with Ignazzio's picture on it. "That's him, isn't it?"

"A few years younger, but yeah. He's a goddamn detective! I told you we shouldn't have come here," Gabby shrieked.

"Stop getting hysterical, for Chrissakes. So what if he's a dick? Better than the FBI. We haven't done anything wrong, anyway."

"No, not much. We're planning to dig up some guy's grave to find money from a bank robbery." Sarcasm dripped off Gabby's words. "Your honor, we didn't know this money was stolen. If you look in the black duffel bag in our bedroom closet back in Newark, you'll see that newspaper article about a bank robbery looks fake. The nice old man who left us all this money wouldn't rob a bank. He was a gentle old soul. He just used a phony name for the hell of it."

Trish reached for Gabby's hand and pulled her close. "Gabby, I know what you think, but if we were doing anything illegal, the FBI would be after us, not some private eye. You need to calm yourself. We have to think clearly. Let's not tell Ignazzio or whatever-his-name-is about the wallet. We'll have dinner with him and then take the bus home tomorrow and forget about the money up here. You're right. We have plenty. We don't need more."

"What do we do with this stuff, his license and all?"

Before Trish could answer her, the phone rang. "Hi, this is

Ignazzio. Something's come up, and I need to change our plans for supper. Is it okay if we meet at the diner instead of the restaurant I told you about?"

"Yeah, sure. We'll meet you there at six. This probably works out better anyway. We want to make it an early night so we can catch the eight-thirty bus tomorrow."

Gabby's eyes were like two big question marks. "What gives?" she asked, after Trish hung up the phone.

"We're meeting him at the diner. He said something came up."

"Yeah, like he can't drive without a license, and he probably has no money since we have his wallet. Give me that thing." Gabby fished inside the wallet and pulled out a wad of soggy bills. She counted out two hundred forty-one dollars. "Do detectives make a lot of money? I don't know anybody who carries around this much cash. We might have to pay for his dinner tonight. He must be going nuts trying to figure out where he lost it."

"At least now we know why his fake accent rolled in and out like the tide. He's as Italian as I am, the phony bastard."

"And he's not from here, which would explain why he's not dressed for the weather. I'm wondering if he carries a gun. Maybe that's why he wouldn't take his jacket off when he was sweating like a pig. Tonight when we leave him, let's both hug him and feel under his arms for a gun."

"This might be fun." Neither of them believed that, but it provided the possibility of some needed comic relief.

Chapter Twelve

STILL PLAYING THE role of the phony Italian gentleman, Irwin Greenberg stood when the women approached his booth in the diner. "Thanks for agreeing to the change in plans for tonight. I appreciate it."

"Yeah, what happened?" Gabby asked.

"Oh, some stuff I wouldn't bore you with, but it's all taken care of. So, are you still giving up the search for Nicolo's money? I wish you'd stay a couple more days. We might get lucky."

"Nope. Gotta get back to Newark before we freeze to death. Besides, we don't get paid if we don't work. If we found a million smackers in the cemetery, we wouldn't care, but it looks like we're still a couple of working girls."

"Did Nicolo say there was a million dollars?"

"No, I made that up," Trish answered.

"I thought maybe if you left me his note, I could keep checking and let you know if I find anything."

"You mean the note I burned up in the ashtray in our room?" Gabby asked.

"Why'd you do that?" he snapped.

Trish looked at Gabby and returned her smirk with one of her own. "No point in keeping it," she said. "I'm sure he wrote it to be funny. Looks like he got the last laugh. He got us into a church, and there's no money."

In a somber tone Ignazzio said, "I guess we should look at the menus." He held his in front of his face as if to shield himself from any more bad news.

During supper, Gabby and Trish peppered him with questions they'd already asked just to see if he gave the same answers. By rough count, Trish estimated he batted about seven-fifty. When the waitress asked if they wanted separate checks, Ignazzio jumped on it. He'd chosen the cheapest thing on the dinner menu, a hot turkey sandwich platter that cost less than a dollar with a drink and dessert.

After paying the checks, Trish asked, "Can you give us a lift to the motel?"

"I'd love to, but I walked over. I'll ask the owner to call a cab for you."

Trish and Gabby waited in the vestibule for the taxi. "Want us to drop you at your place?" Trish asked Ignazzio.

He patted his ample stomach. "I need the exercise, but thanks."

Before walking out to the taxi, Trish turned to him. "I guess this is goodbye. Thanks for all your help." She reached over and hugged him, feeling for a gun holster under his bulky sweater.

Gabby did the same. "Arrivederci, Ignazzio," she said and released him.

"You girls be careful and have a safe trip home." He waved as their taxi pulled away.

"I'll give him one thing," Gabby said. "The bastard's smooth. How'd you like him asking for Mr. C's note?"

"Yeah, like I'd be so stupid. What a pisser."

BACK AT THE motel, they stopped at the office to settle their bill. While Trish waited for the clerk to make a copy, Gabby wandered to the window and called out, "Babe, c'mere."

"What is it? I'm almost done here."

"Some guy who looked a lot like Ignazzio went into the room next to ours," she whispered.

"You sure? You're half blind."

"Not positive, but it sure looked like him."

Trish asked the clerk, "You got somebody named Guarino staying here?"

The young man said, "Give me a minute," and disappeared into the office.

The woman who'd checked them in came over to Trish. "Are you leaving us so soon, Miss Mulkern? May I help you with something?"

"Wondering if you have a guest named Guarino staying here. He's a friend, and he said he might be in town when we were."

"No, I'd remember the name. Nobody here by that name." She quickly traded her welcoming smile for a frown and a clenched jaw.

"Well, we'll be off for home in the morning. Thanks for everything."

The smile returned. "Just drop your key on the desk before you leave tomorrow. Have a safe trip."

Gabby and Trish entered their room with entirely different ideas of how to spend their last evening in Gloversville. Trish slipped off her jacket and put her finger to her lips. She turned on the TV and cranked up the volume. She took Gabby's hand and led her into the bathroom.

"What's going on?"

"Talk softly. If he's next door, he can probably hear us talking. The bitch at the desk is lying. I could tell by her face. Did you notice how fast the kid at the desk disappeared when I mentioned a guest named Guarino? Something weird's going on in this place. She must be in cahoots with Ignazzio, or Greenberg, or whatever the hell his name is."

"You got any matches?" Gabby asked.

"No. Why?"

"Cause the minute we leave here tomorrow, I bet he'll be in here looking for the burnt up note. Give me some change."

"What are you gonna do, hire a cheap arsonist?" Trish handed Gabby her loose change.

"I'll be right back." Gabby returned with a pack of Chesterfields and matches. "I've got an idea. Let's put a note in the ashtray telling Irwin Greenberg where he can find his wallet. We can stick it under the mattress so he can get it after we leave. I don't want to be accused of stealing the guy's wallet."

Trish grabbed Gabby and kissed her. "Brilliant! That way he'll know we're on to him and maybe he'll leave us alone. We can singe the edges of the note but leave the message so he can read it."

They had to do the note twice because Gabby burned the first one up by mistake and threw it in the toilet to avoid setting the place on fire. "Now can we leave the bathroom?" Gabby still hoped they could salvage another romantic night, but knowing Ignazzio might be next door listening, Trish wasn't interested.

Trish pushed the chair in front of the door and they watched TV until they fell asleep.

"IT'S TIME TO get up," Gabby called from the club chair in front of the door. "I can't believe you slept. I might have gotten maybe two hours and then I was wide awake."

"That's a switch. Did you shower?"

"Nope. Going home dirty."

Trish pushed the covers off and trotted to the bathroom. "I'll be fast. Put the TV on."

Gabby switched channels until she found her favorite cartoon program, one she'd watched when she was trying to perfect her English.

Dressed and packed, Trish called, "Come over here and help me with the mattress."

They slipped the wallet underneath and Gabby pushed it in as far as her arm would reach. "Let the bastard struggle to find it."

Gabby moved the chair away from the door and left the TV on so their neighbor would think they were still in the room. They then tiptoed past his door.

There wasn't much in the office to salvage for breakfast except donuts, so they each took two and wrapped them in napkins before slipping them into their purses. The bus would stop in Albany for twenty minutes and they planned to get coffee there. That would hold them until they got to Newark.

"Can you call us a taxi?" Trish asked the kid at the desk.

"I'm relieved to be out of there," Gabby said, once they were in the taxi. "I kept expecting trouble."

"Yeah, me too. I'll be happy to see Newark again."

They looked around while waiting for the driver to signal them to board the bus. He talked to someone on his walkie-talkie and seemed to be looking their way. Trish's heart pounded as he got out of his seat and opened the door. "Good morning, ladies." He motioned to their bag. "Want to take it on with you, or should I stow it?"

"Stow it," Gabby replied.

They climbed aboard and since they were the only passengers, they took two seats apiece across the aisle from one another. They remembered most of the passengers had gotten off in Albany on the trip up and wanted to enjoy extra space until they piled on for the return trip.

The bus inched away from the station and Trish's shoulders

relaxed. She looked across at Gabby, who was retrieving a donut from her shoulder bag. For the first time in three days, she believed their weird experience was over. At least, she hoped so.

With each mile between them and Gloversville, Trish felt more at ease. They drank cold coffee and munched on donuts that had lost most of their powdered sugar and cinnamon in their purses. Gabby made up for lost sleep by dozing periodically on Trish's shoulder. Only two more stops before Newark.

Gray, dilapidated Penn Station looked mighty good to them. They splurged and took a cab home. Trish stopped at the mailbox to retrieve an accumulation of junk mail. Gabby had the apartment door open by the time she got there and smiled broadly as she held something out to her.

It was Irwin Greenberg's card with a note on the back. He'd scribbled, "You girls are all right. Thought I'd stop by and say thanks on my way back to Philadelphia. Ciao." He signed it IG.

"Where'd you find this?"

Gabby pointed to the metal ring around the peephole in their door. "It was stuck in here."

"I guess he found the note and the wallet. I was right. He was in cahoots with the motel manager. She must have let him into our room after we left. He would have gotten here faster than our bus if he didn't stop. Let's hope we've seen the last of him."

Gabby nodded. "Yeah, good riddance."

Chapter Thirteen

"BOY, YOUR UNCLE has more lives than a cat," Rosalie said. "Back from death's door, huh? I'm sure you're relieved. Must have been my prayers."

"You really believe in all that praying stuff, Ro?"

Rosalie looked around to be sure they were alone. "Look, I live with a guy who kicks the crap out of me when he has to pay out more than he takes in from numbers, or when the goombahs treat him like the low-life he is. If it wasn't for them, he probably would have killed me by now. They need the money he brings in from numbers, and he knows it, so even though they look out for me, there are plenty of times they don't see the bruises. You know what I'm saying?"

"That's my point. If there was a God, would he let that happen to you?"

"Maybe. I done some shit in my time. Maybe this is payback. I think it would be worse if I didn't pray. I need to believe in something so it might as well be God. I'm serious. Maybe my prayers helped your uncle."

"He said I was the best medicine he could have had. Within two days he asked when he could go home." Trish looked at her friend and said, "Ro, I need to tell you..."

"What?"

"Never mind." Trish slinked off to the diner kitchen.

Trish worked half a day before the boss arrived. He caught her between trips to the kitchen and took her hand. "I'm so sorry..."

"Not yet, but thanks," she said. "He's still alive. I don't know how long he'll last, but when the time comes I'll have to go back up there."

"Sure, sure. No problem. I hope it's not for a long time. My mother was like that. One minute, the doctors said she was at death's door, and the next minute he said she had another five or six months. That went on for two years. Most of the time, she wasn't in pain and she was home with my sisters, so we were grateful."

"I know exactly how you feel," several of the girls said, and Trish wished she could tell them how very wrong they were.

Gabby and Trish took their supper break after the evening rush. "You know, it actually feels good to be back at work. It feels more normal. Weird, huh?" Trish said.

Gabby pointed to Trish's plate that was piled high with a hot turkey sandwich, mashed potatoes, and cranberry sauce. "You thinking of Ignazzio?"

Trish laughed. "Not consciously."

"I'd love to know who he was working for. Who the hell hired him to follow us around?"

"We'll probably never know. Whoever it was sure wasted their money. Maybe he didn't even get paid since he didn't come up with the dough."

A few days after they got home they counted the money in the black bag and it was all there. "We need to put this someplace," Gabby said.

"Like where? I don't think we can waltz into a bank with ninety-five thousand dollars in cash and open an account. The cops would be all over us like flies on horseshit."

"Doesn't Rosalie's husband run numbers?" Gabby asked. "What's he do with his cash?"

"Probably keeps it in the sugar jar, the asshole. He's not too swift. I'll ask Rosalie if I can figure out a way to do it without telling her anything. Let me think about it."

DURING A LULL after lunch a few days later, Rosalie told Trish she and Sean were going down the shore for two weeks next summer. "He says we're gonna rent a house on Long Beach Island with five bedrooms. It's real expensive, but he says not to worry about it. He says we're gonna eat out every night, so I don't have to cook. He's being nice to me all of a sudden. You know what that means."

"You think he's got somebody on the side?"

"I hope so. I'm sure he hit big on the numbers for a few months, so if he wants to act like a big shot, I'm okay with it as long as he don't give me the clap."

"Aren't you afraid somebody's gonna break into your apartment and steal the money?"

"Nah, he does what the bookies do. They buy traveler's checks. Nobody can trace it and you can spend them anywhere."

Trish laughed. "Great idea. I never gave him credit for being that smart."

"Oh, yeah. When it comes to money, he's a regular Einstein."

During her bus ride home, Trish mulled over what Rosalie had told her. As soon as she entered their apartment, she called to Gabby, "Traveler's checks."

"What about them?"

"That's what Rosalie's husband does with his cash. It's what all the bookies do."

"I never bought traveler's checks. How do you get them?" Gabby asked.

"I don't know, but it can't be too complicated. Tomorrow, I'll take a couple of hundred dollars to the bank down the street and find out."

"RIGHT THIS WAY, Miss Mulkern. A man in an ill-fitting blue suit led Trish into a glass-enclosed office off the main floor of the Howard Savings Bank. "Do you have an account with us?"

"Do I have to?"

"Oh no, we can sell traveler's checks to anyone. How much money in checks do you wish to purchase?"

"Two hundred dollars." Trish reached into her wallet and drew two bills out.

"And how do you want them? I'd suggest smaller checks because some places don't want to cash them if they're larger than twenty dollars."

"That's fine." Trish suppressed a nervous cough. "I'm sure people in Ireland will be fine with that." She'd already mentioned a trip to her ancestral home.

The banker returned and placed ten, twenty-dollar traveler's checks in front of her. Pointing to the top line, he handed her a pen and said to sign her name. As she signed each check, he explained, "You don't sign the bottom until you're ready to cash them. That way, if a thief steals the checks, they'll have to forge your signature." He handed her a check register. "Put the numbers in here so you can keep track of them."

Trish left the bank amazed at how easy it was to get rid of cash legally without having to spend it.

To avoid suspicion, Trish and Gabby estimated they'd have to repeat the process four hundred seventy-five times to convert all of the cash, unless they did five hundred dollars at a time.

"That's a lotta damn banks," Gabby said. I don't know if there are that many in Newark."

"If we each do it, that'll cut the amount in half," Trish suggested.

"Oh, right. I can see them calling the cops when a Puerto Rican chick comes in with five hundred bucks. They'll think I stole it."

Trish wanted to argue but knew Gabby had a point.

Gabby scribbled on a piece of scrap paper. "If we hit three or four banks a week, it'll only take eight or nine months. Hey, how about money orders? That's how I sent money to my family. I could get them in your name, and you could get them in mine. You have to pay, but it might be worth it not to have to find so many banks."

"Do rich people have to go through this?" Trish asked.

"I never knew having a lot of money could be such a pain in the ass. No wonder Mr. C kept cash. Except that we both know he might have done it for other reasons," Gabby said.

Over the next several weeks, Gabby and Trish visited a myriad of banks and every drugstore and grocery that sold money orders. With the collection of traveler's checks and money orders safely squirreled away in the black bag, they felt a bit less vulnerable, but still looked over their shoulders before unlocking their apartment door.

Chapter Fourteen

TRISH STOPPED IN her tracks when she got home after a late shift and spied an empty bottle of Four Roses on the kitchen table. Gabby dozed in a chair in front of the TV.

"Wake up. Have you been drinking this?" Trish held the nearly empty bottle. "Last time I saw it, it was half full. You drank all that?"

"I'll replace it. Don't get hysterical."

Trish turned off the TV.

"I think you're missing my point," she said through clenched teeth. "You rarely drank the whole time I've known you, and now you polished off half a bottle of whiskey? What gives? You becoming a boozer?"

"Plenty of people drink that much in a night. You should know from your parents."

"We're not talking about my parents, but since you brought them up, if they hadn't thrown me out, I'd have moved out because of their drinking. Maybe I have to remind you how much I hate it."

Trish hadn't given much weight to Gabby telling her she'd been a party girl in Puerto Rico. When she said she drank rum and Coke the way people in New Jersey drank plain Cokes, Trish assumed that was a Puerto Rican tradition.

Trish remembered how drunk Gabby had gotten in Gloversville after a couple of glasses of wine and wondered. She took the bottle into the kitchen and poured the rest of the whiskey down the drain. Then she climbed on the stepladder and stretched to reach the shelf above the refrigerator. She couldn't see the shelf, but slid her hand across the surface searching for the other bottle of whiskey.

"It's not there," Gabby said from the doorway behind Trish.

Trish twisted around to see Gabby's tear-stained face.

"Where is it?"

"Where do you think?" she sobbed. "I think I need to see somebody about my nerves, babe." She held up her glass filled with ice and a trace of whiskey. "This is the only thing that helps me relax lately."

"You mean like a psychiatrist?"

Gabby snapped, "I'm not nuts, just nervous. It's all this money and worrying about your safety and the cops..."

Trish walked over and took the glass out of her hand. She wrapped her arms around Gabby and they cried together.

"I know you're not nuts, but this could be a sickness. How long has it been going on?"

Trish kicked herself for not questioning why Gabby began binging on mints, and for accepting her explanation that she used them to settle a sour stomach.

"Not long...a couple of weeks...but it's not the first time."

"What do you mean?" Trish let go and said, "Let's talk. No yelling. No accusing. I want you to tell me everything."

For half an hour, Gabby talked while Trish listened. By the end of the conversation, Trish knew two things: Gabby had a serious drinking problem when she was fifteen; and she stayed sober long enough to know she had the strength to do it again.

They hugged and cried several more times that night before Trish extracted a promise from Gabby to go to an Alcoholics Anonymous meeting.

"I love you, Gabby, and I'll stand by you as long as you work to get and stay sober."

Trish had never been loved by anyone the way Gabby loved her, but she knew the alcohol monster was a mean devil she wasn't sure she wanted to deal with again.

THE NEXT MORNING, Trish heard Gabby on the phone talking with a friend they hadn't seen in a while. Roberta was a recovering alcoholic and from the bits and pieces Trish overheard, it sounded like Gabby was getting information about a local meeting. Before leaving for her morning shift, Trish put on enough makeup to cover the dark circles under her eyes. She bent down for a goodbye kiss and interrupted Gabby who was reading the morning paper. Gabby casually announced, "I'm going to an AA meeting this morning at the Presbyterian church with Roberta."

"Great, babe," Trish said, and barely resisted the temptation to do cartwheels across the apartment.

A week later, Trish said, "I am very proud of you for going to four AA meetings. We should make this Christmas a special celebration. It might be our last in Newark. How about we each take a hundred dollars of Mr. C's money and buy some special presents for each other?"

"We can make Christmas lists like we did when we were kids!" Gabby said.

"That's a great idea. Does it matter if we were naughty or nice?" Trish asked.

Gabby lowered her eyelids to half-mast and batted her eyelashes. "This Santa likes naughty girls, so let's see how naughty you can be in the next week."

"Can we start now?" Trish knew Gabby wasn't due at work for a few hours. She tugged her arm and pulled her toward the bedroom.

After making love, they showered together to save time and Gabby jumped into her uniform and tore out of the apartment to catch the bus. Trish wasn't due until the supper shift, so she had plenty of time to contemplate her Christmas list.

It was hard to keep the awful memories of Christmases of her childhood at bay. Images of drunken parents, her father throwing the Christmas tree out the window and eating Oreos in church with the other kids on Christmas afternoon after her oldest brother rescued them from the insanity in their apartment.

Trish forced those dark thoughts from her mind and focused on her list. She smiled picturing Gabby going into one of the expensive downtown department stores to shop with Mr. C's money. Her list was short, with a portable radio in the number one spot, and a gold locket second. It was fun imagining she might get one of them.

Gabby made a list during her break and slipped it into the pocket of Trish's uniform as they greeted each other briefly before she left the diner. Trish laughed when she saw the red Caddy with a singing horn atop Gabby's list. Next on the list were diamond earrings followed by genuine leather knee-length boots and a watch.

TRISH HAD PARTIAL success pushing Gloversville out of

her mind until five days before Christmas. She woke up from a dream that morning with a crystal clear image of one of the stained glass windows in the Church of the Holy Spirit. It was the one with the white dove, and in her dream, the feet were especially prominent. She didn't recall noticing the feet when they were in the church, but in her dream she'd exclaimed to Gabby, "Look, the bird has three toes and they look like fingers."

"So?"

"Tredita."

"You think?"

Trish took Mr. C's letter from her jewelry box and reread the last paragraph. It was as mysterious to her as the first several times she'd read it, but now the part about Tredita took on new meaning.

TRISH GREETED GABBY at the apartment door that evening. "Turn your Puerto Rican ESP on."

"Uh oh. What'd you lose this time?" Gabby hesitated in the doorway.

Trish pulled her into the apartment babbling about her dream. She stopped when she noted worry lines deepening on Gabby's brow.

"Whoa, Trish. Rewind, but let me take off my coat first." She threw her coat over a dinette chair. "Okay, now start over and slow down." She listened to Trish's story. "You're not thinking of going back there, are you? Because if you are, I'm going to tie you to the bed. Better yet, I'll get handcuffs."

"No, of course not," Trish answered hastily. "It's just that I thought..."

"Don't think. Not about that place. I'm aiming for my one-month sobriety token, and I don't want to go down that road again."

"Okay, okay." Trish tried to forget the dream with little success but did not mention it to Gabby again.

SHE TURNED HER attention to shopping. After spending hours looking at gifts that were far more expensive than she'd imagined, she purchased a watch and small diamond studs for

Gabby. She wished she could find a toy Cadillac and was about to give up when she walked into a hobby shop and saw one. Unfortunately, it was a kit that required assembly.

"Is this hard to put together?" she asked the clerk.

"Not if you know what you're doing. Ever done one?"

Trish shook her head. The skinny guy with a short black mustache suddenly took on a potbelly and full white beard like Santa Claus when he asked, "Want me to put it together for you?"

"Oh, would you?"

"I love to tinker with those things, but I can't do it today. Can you come back in a day or two?"

"Name the day and I'll be here."

Filled with Christmas spirit, Trish left the shop and walked to the bus stop. Of all the days to find the crankiest driver in Newark at the wheel. He scowled as Trish deposited her coins into the money slot. She put on her best smile and said, "I hope you get everything you deserve for Christmas," and reached for the overhead bar before the bus shot out into traffic. She imagined he'd love to see her go flying, but she was determined to deny him that perverse pleasure.

THE DINER NEVER closed on holidays. For many years before she had met Gabby, Trish volunteered to work on Christmas so the girls with kids could be off. She was amazed at how many people came in alone. She tried to be especially nice to them and bought several large Santa-decorated cookies to give to them. This year, she and Gabby had off on Christmas, so they cooked dinner for the single girls who were off, and for the others who dropped by after their shifts. Gabby made a turkey and ham and Trish took care of the side dishes. There were seven for dinner plus Rosalie, who managed to sneak away from her in-laws in time for dessert.

The tiny artificial tree with the bent stand stood on top of the TV propped up by the rabbit ears antenna. The women ate on their laps and listened to Christmas music on Trish's new portable radio.

After they left, Trish put on her gold locket and Gabby decked herself out in her diamond studs and watch. They stood together in front of the full-length mirror on the closet door and admired their gifts.

"One day, babe, we won't have to hide and lie anymore. It's wearing me down lying to our friends. The scary thing is that I do it so easily I almost don't have to think about it anymore."

"It's not like we're lying to hurt anybody," Gabby reflected. "We're lying so nobody, including us, gets hurt."

"Yeah, all those years Mr. C had this money, but couldn't do anything with it to make himself feel good. I hope he's watching from wherever he is and knows we did something nice for each other. He'd like that."

Chapter Fifteen

TRISH TRIED HARD to shake the dream about the stained glass window, but despite her efforts, she dreamed it again on New Year's Day. She couldn't blame it on a hangover since she and Gabby spent New Year's Eve eating Chinese food and drinking Cokes. They stayed up to watch Guy Lombardo's Orchestra, and twirled around the living room imitating the rich people dancing at The Roosevelt Grill in New York. They counted down the last seconds of 1953 and watched the ball drop in Times Square. Gabby made a list of all the good things that happened in 1953 and it was quite a long list. Except for a debate about whether Margaret O'Donnell's marriage belonged on the list, they agreed on everything.

They kept their New Year's resolutions brief. Gabby resolved to earn her one-year sobriety coin, and Trish repeated her annual resolution to lose weight. Jointly, they resolved not to fight, to quit their diner jobs by the end of the year, and use Mr. C's money to move someplace nice.

The one about not fighting was short-lived when Trish had another dream about the church in Gloversville, and believed it contained a clue. She wasn't positive, but she was pretty sure she remembered a painting of San Salvador in the church. He was the saint who performed miraculous cures.

Once, when she asked Mr. C why he chose to call himself Salvatore, instead of Sal, he told her it was because he felt drawn to the saint who was orphaned at a young age.

"But your parents didn't die when you were a boy."

"True, Patricia, but I left them, which is worse than if they died. I knew I could never see them again." Another puzzling statement, Trish thought.

Trish smacked her forehead with the heel of her hand after an inadvertent slip about the dream at supper one night.

"You're not starting that shit again, are you?" Gabby asked.

"Oh, your Puerto Rican ESP is fine and dandy, but my dreams are shit?"

The argument raged for nearly an hour until Trish went into the bedroom and put on a Montovani record. She lay on the bed and closed her eyes. While she listened, she tried to imagine Mr. C as a young boy in the Church of the Holy Spirit, gazing at the painting of San Salvador.

Trish wasn't sure where the painting was. It might be on the wall with the stained glass window of the Holy Spirit, but there were times when she visualized it on the opposite side. She wished she had taken a camera.

When Trish wasn't sleeping and dreaming about Gloversville, she obsessed about the meaning of the dreams. She wished Gabby didn't get so agitated when she brought them up. She could use her detective brain, not to mention her ESP.

Many nights, Trish lay awake staring at the ceiling, wondering if everybody in the building except Gabby was also listening to the world's loudest hissing radiators. Some nights, when it was especially windy, the wind whistled through the bottom of the vestibule door. Too many times during the night she'd gone out to be sure it was closed.

One afternoon at work, Rosalie asked, "Did you go a few rounds with Rocky Marciano?" No amount of makeup masked Trish's circles beneath her circles.

Even her boss asked one too many times, "Are you okay?"

"I'm worried about my Uncle Paddy."

"Still hanging on, huh?"

"Yeah, I guess he's not ready to go. The doctors don't know what's keeping him alive. He's some kind of medical miracle."

Some miracle. The real miracle was that so far, Gabby and Trish hadn't screwed up all the lies they told to different people. Gabby caught Trish staring at her image in front of a mirror one day and when she asked what was wrong, Trish answered, "I'm not sure I know who that is."

Chapter Sixteen

"WHERE SHOULD WE look for a new place?" Gabby asked.

"Do we want to stay in New Jersey?"

"Not Newark, for sure. I want to live somewhere pretty, like we said on New Year's Eve."

Trish took the Rand McNally Atlas of the United States out and flipped through it to find the map of the entire country and spread it out. "I really hate the heat," she said, "so Florida, Georgia, Alabama, Louisiana, and Mississippi are definitely out."

"I don't want to live with cowboys, so Texas is out, too," Gabby said.

By the time they'd eliminated various states, they realized they knew nothing about the remaining ones.

ON THEIR NEXT day off, they took a bus downtown to the main library. They hesitated as they viewed the imposing columned façade, so they sat on a bench in the small park across the street.

"All those people going in look really smart," Gabby said. "They're gonna think we're a couple of dummies. Do you know how to find anything in there?"

"I was only in there once in high school, but I don't remember anything about it."

After a few minutes, Trish pulled Gabby by her coat sleeve. "C'mon, we're going in. Somebody will help us find books about the states."

They dodged cars and made their way across Washington Street and up the marble steps.

"Whoa. Look at those naked guys," Gabby said, pointing to the carving above the door. "Do you have to take your clothes off inside?"

"You'd be happy to go in if that was true, wouldn't you?"

"With guys? Hell, no."

Gabby hung back while Trish approached the information

desk. She returned with a map and directions to the second floor reference department.

Between them, they carried a dozen books to a long, time-worn wooden table where several people sat reading.

"Look up," Gabby said, in a too-loud voice prompting a couple of people to shush her. Trish put her finger to her lips and tilted her head back to see a beautiful stained glass panel in the center of the domed ceiling.

"I wonder if this used to be a church," Trish said, and Gabby promptly put her finger to her lips. They laughed and ignored a squinty-eyed glare from an elderly man across from them.

Trish removed a stack of scrap paper slips from her coat pocket and wrote on one of them, "If you find anything interesting, put one of these on the page." She dove into a large book on California with vivid photos and after a few minutes looked up to see that Gabby hadn't opened a book. She nudged Gabby and pointed to the stack of books. Gabby shrugged and smiled while framing her fingers around her eyes and shaking her head. Trish sighed.

Gabby got up to look at paintings on the walls while Trish read. It took so long to get through the chapter on San Francisco that she knew it would take months to cover the remaining states.

Trish used her temporary card to check out five books. On the way down the front steps she groused, "This is going to take forever."

"All I care about is being near a big airport so I can get flights to San Juan," Gabby said.

A FIERCE WIND threatened to tear the books out of Trish's hands, so she hugged them to her chest. "You got change for the bus? I can't get into my purse."

Trish noticed a young woman on the other side of the bus stop sign watching her. She didn't even avert her eyes when Trish stared back. She carried a briefcase and wore a blue car coat with a fake fur collar that looked like it belonged to somebody a lot bigger. Trish turned away but looked back every few minutes. "Do you know that girl?" she asked Gabby.

After a few more minutes of the visual game of chicken, the woman approached and asked, "Trish?"

"Do I know you?" Trish snarled.

"It's me, Mary."

"Did we go to school together?"

The woman hesitated before saying, "Only when you took me."

Trish's breath caught in her throat. "Oh, my God. Little Mary?"

Mary nodded and wiped at her eyes with a glove.

Gabby watched with curiosity until Trish turned to her and said, "Mary is my sister."

"This is Gabby, my girlfriend."

Trish eyed the approaching bus and felt relief to see it was hers. "Well, here's my bus. I have to go. Nice to see you."

Gabby got on first and paid their fares. The driver started to close the door when Mary stuck her arm between the rubber halves forcing it open, and got on. Trish followed Gabby to a double seat and handed her the books before sitting down. Mary walked up the aisle and stood next to Trish.

"I couldn't let you walk out of my life again," she said, tears welling on her lower lids. She took a seat behind them.

Gabby nudged Trish and pointed with her head. Trish got up slowly and spoke to Mary. "There are two seats together back there. Do you want to sit with me?"

Mary smiled and walked behind Trish. Trish felt suddenly light-headed and grabbed for the overhead bar. They sat.

"Where do you live?" Trish asked. She recognized the address and knew it was on the other side of Newark. "Why'd you get on this bus?"

"I told you. I couldn't bear to lose you again. I knew if I didn't get on this bus, I might never find you. I saw you in the library and knew right away it was you. Your face hasn't changed in all these years."

Trish laughed and looked down. "'Can't say that for the rest of me."

"Do you have any idea how important you were and still are to me? You were more of a mother to me than anyone. I remember how you'd come home from school and get upset when you'd find me wearing dirty clothes and looking like a street waif. You gave me bubble baths and washed and ironed my clothes. You were the one who took the time to sit and read to me, and tell me stories. It was you the principal called to come and take me home when I wet my pants in first grade, not our mother. I've never forgotten you, Trish. Your kindness told me I was worth something. Every time I had to make a decision about my life, I imagined talking with you about it. I knew I'd find you again one day."

Gabby turned every so often to check on Trish. She smiled to let her know she was okay.

Mary filled Trish in on the family. Their father had died two years after he threw her out, and their mother went on welfare. They moved to the projects and, with financial help from the oldest three who'd left before Trish, they managed. Mary was the last one left at home until two years earlier, when she got a scholarship to Rutgers and moved in with her boyfriend's family. She hadn't had much contact with their mother but told Trish Mrs. Mulkern had pretty much stopped drinking with the help of AA.

"Did she ever talk about me?" Trish surprised herself with the question.

"Not when he was around," Mary answered. "A couple of times I asked her if we could go see you, and she smacked me. I finally quit asking."

"I sent a Christmas card and never heard back. I guess it didn't get forwarded after all these years," Trish said softly.

Gabby stood as they approached their stop. Trish looked at Mary. "We get off here. You want to stop in?"

"If it's okay with Gabby."

"She'll be fine. C'mon."

"LET ME TAKE your coat," Gabby said as Mary stood looking around the living room. She wiggled out of her coat and handed it to Gabby. Her eyes were drawn immediately to one object on an end table. She walked over and picked up the snow globe she'd saved up to give Trish for Christmas the last year Trish lived at home.

"You saved this," she whispered as Trish approached her. Her eyes glistened as she put it back on the table.

"It's the only thing I still have from home," Trish answered. "When the old man told me to pack my stuff and get out, I ran into the bedroom and grabbed my clothes and stuffed them into a shopping bag. I remember looking around the room and thinking that I didn't want anything else, but then I saw the snow globe you gave me and put it in the bag. I've thought of you every time I looked at it." Trish's voice broke and she quickly turned away from Mary.

Mary picked up the globe again and cradling it in her hands, she said, "I scrounged empty soda bottles I found in the garbage and turned them in to the deli down the street until I got enough to buy this for you. It took a lot of bottles at two cents apiece, but I finally saved enough and went into the store and put all of my money on the counter. I was a little short but the lady said I could buy it if I promised to come back with the few cents when I got it."

Trish turned back to face Mary. "It was the best gift anybody ever gave me and you were so excited that you didn't even wait till Christmas. I remember you gave it to me the day before." She smiled and took the globe from Mary's hands. "It's gone with me everywhere I've lived."

"I did go back with the six cents I owed the lady, by the way."

Trish returned the globe to the table. "I don't know what you paid for it, but to me, it's priceless."

"Do you mind if I hug you?" Mary asked.

Trish reached her arms out and Mary stepped into her embrace.

"You guys are going to make me cry," Gabby said. "How about a cup of coffee?"

"I really need to get home," Mary answered. "I have a test tomorrow and I need to study. Can I have a rain check?"

"Of course. I'll walk you to the bus stop," Trish said. "But first, let me have your phone number and I'll give you mine."

TRISH AND MARY spoke by phone several times during the next week. Reconnecting with her sister absorbed nearly all of Trish's focus as she tried to get to know the woman she'd last seen as a young child.

"You seem like a sweet, innocent person. I can't believe you were raised in such a mess."

Mary caught Trish up on which of their siblings had ended up in the juvenile justice system and Trish shook her head. "I'm glad you escaped that life."

"Actually, I didn't," Mary said. "When I was in ninth grade, a friend and I robbed a store."

"Oh, God," Trish gasped.

"Every time I needed something, I went to Mom and she said she didn't have any money. Things were so tight, there were times all we had for supper was baked beans or mashed potatoes. I knew it was wrong to steal but we were hungry, so I talked a friend into helping me get some food. Like two idiots, we got caught. We might have gotten away with it if my friend didn't drop a package of bacon on our way out of the store. The owner chased us down the street, and we dropped everything we'd lifted by the time he grabbed me."

"The son of a bitch called the cops?"

"Yeah, we cried and begged him not to, but he did."

"You were what, thirteen or fourteen?"

"Yeah, fourteen. Thank God for Richard. He got my teachers to write letters about what a good student I was and came to court with me. Mom wouldn't come. The hearing officer read all the letters and said she'd give me a second chance. She said if I got into any kind of trouble, in school or out, she'd send me to juvie."

"How're you gonna get a teaching job with that on your record?"

"When you turn eighteen, if you've kept your nose clean, they wipe out the record. Believe me, I was so terrified that I was probably the best-behaved kid in school."

"What about your friend?"

"She got the same deal but ended up pregnant and dropped out of school. I heard her family moved."

"If anybody else had told me this, I'd have said they were lying."

"Don't judge me, Trish. It's not like I stole money or jewelry. In my twisted kid's mind, I thought I'd be helping the family. Of course, Mom didn't see it that way. She nearly beat me to death. Richard saved my butt again. I miss him so much. You and he were like my parents."

"Where is Richard?"

"I thought I told you. He was killed in Korea. I'm sorry, Trish. They say the good die young. He was proof of that. If any of us turned out good, it was because of him."

Trish shook her head. "What a shame. I'm not judging you, honey. Just surprised, is all. It's probably a good thing you got caught. You might have gone on to worse things."

"Eventually, that's how I came to see it, too. I spent so much time in church saying the Rosary that I even thought of becoming a nun. That's how guilty I felt."

"That would have been worse than going to jail. I'm glad you changed your mind. Are you still religious?"

"Some. I still go to church on holidays, but I'm not sure how much I still believe. How about you?"

"Nah. Once I found out the priest turned our parents against me for being queer, that was it. I don't go where I'm not wanted."

"YOU THINK MARY'S okay with us?" Gabby asked one evening. "She knows why your parents threw you out, doesn't she?"

"Yeah, she knows now. I told her. She still wants us to meet her boyfriend, so I guess she's okay with it."

"I worry about you. I don't want you to get hurt if she gets weird. I can see you're getting close to her. Just be careful."

Trish put her arms around Gabby's shoulders. "How the hell did I get so lucky? The day you walked into Scotty's was the best day of my life. If I ever get wind of something like that, I'll cut her off. If I learned one thing after getting tossed out, it's that I'm never taking that shit from anybody again. That includes Mary."

JANUARY WAS THE coldest month Trish could remember. She and Gabby dipped into the black bag and took out money to buy new hooded coats and the warmest mittens they could find. Trish was never impressed with fur coats, thinking they looked better on animals, but there were days when she was tempted.

Twice they had to cancel plans to visit Mary at her boyfriend's place because of ice.

"You think maybe we're not intended to meet the boyfriend?" Trish asked, after the second cancellation.

"Stop with the superstition," Gabby scolded. "We'll meet him in the spring."

After Mary told them his name, Otilio, Gabby was eager to meet a fellow Puerto Rican.

Mary and Trish managed to meet downtown for coffee a couple of times and Mary told her that the other kids had no interest in meeting her. Mary shared the irony that the news of Richard's death is what pushed their mother to go to AA and quit drinking. Trish took some comfort in the hope that their brother, wherever he might be, knew his death had produced something positive.

The late afternoon sun cast a glow over the side of Harris's Cafeteria where Trish and Mary sat. Flecks of dust danced in the rays that shone on their table. Mary stared into the distance.

"Trish...Could you have gotten on the bus that day and never seen me again?"

Trish put her cup down and sloshed coffee in the saucer. She stared at Mary while she pondered her response.

"To tell the truth, I think I was in shock when you came over and talked to me. After our parents threw me out, I must have cried every night for a year. I don't know if you remember when I came to the schoolyard and saw you kids. When you told me they beat you for talking to me, I knew I had to keep away. Believe me, if I had a decent job, I'd have tried to get you out of there, but I barely made enough to survive." Trish licked her spoon and stared into her cup. "To be honest, I probably could have ridden off if you hadn't gotten on, but I might have regretted it for the rest of my life." Trish reached over and took Mary's hands in hers. "I'm sorry, little sister, but I hope you understand that's the best I can do. I'm happy you're back in my life, but there's always the nagging thought that someday you'll say you're ashamed of me and push me away. That's the real damage our parents caused."

Mary squeezed Trish's hands as she spoke and felt her sister's trembling fingers. "That will never happen. I swear to God. It makes me sick to think about how much time we lost not being in touch. I'll never choose to hurt you. Maybe one day you'll be able to believe me."

Chapter Seventeen

GABBY AND TRISH rotated hosting meals with Mary and Otilio, and Gabby and Otilio vied for the honor of making the best Puerto Rican dishes. Otilio declared himself the winner one night after they'd feasted on Mofongo, a delectable dish made with fried plantains stuffed with spicy pork, but Gabby soon wrested the title away from him with an offering of Asopao de Mariscos, a seafood stew. Otilio was gracious in conceding his defeat, but vowed a rematch.

One day, Trish was shocked to see Otilio walk into the diner. She motioned for him to sit at her station and rushed to bring him a menu. When he picked up the menu, it shook. Only his warm smile reassured Trish he was not bringing bad news about Mary.

"What brings you to this neck of the woods?"

"Would you believe me if I said I happened to be in the neighborhood and decided to drop by to say hello?"

"Of course not. What's up?"

Trish tried to ignore the guy at the next booth who kept snapping his fingers. After his third try, she said, "I'll be right with you."

"Go ahead before he stiffs you on the tip," Otilio said.

Trish returned, order pad in hand. "Seriously, is something wrong?"

"No, everything's fine. We're all good. I'll have a BLT and a Coke."

"You must have had a better reason than that to come all this way."

His smile disappeared. "When do you get a break? There's something I need to discuss with you." He reacted quickly to the dark cloud that crossed Trish's face. "Stop worrying. It's good news, I promise."

Trish glanced at the clock. "I get off in half an hour. I can hold off putting in your order if you promise not to complain to my boss."

Otilio drew a cross over his heart. "Sure, but bring my Coke, please. I'll wait for the sandwich."

As soon as Trish's boss left the diner, she slipped off her apron and sat with Otilio while he ate. Between bites, he smiled while Trish tapped her fingers on the table and folded and unfolded the straw wrapper until it fell apart.

Otilio wiped his mouth and pushed his plate away. "I graduate in May," he explained. "I just found out I can have a job where I did my internship, at the *Bergen Record* in Hackensack. It's every journalism major's dream job, and I'm excited about it." He swallowed hard before continuing. "I want to marry Mary so she can come with me." He let out an extended breath. "What do you think?"

"Wow, you caught me by surprise with this one. What does Mary think?"

"She loves me, but she still has two more years to finish her degree. She's not sure she wants to leave school."

"Does she know you're talking to me?"

"Well...she did say she wanted to talk to you before she gives me an answer, but to tell the truth, I wanted to get to you first. So...no, she doesn't know I'm here. I'm hoping you'll help convince her to marry me."

"No way am I getting in the middle of this. You two need to work it out. I'll tell you, Mary's education is very important to her, but you know that. I can see you're eager, but you might have to be patient."

"I suspect that's what she'll say, too. Two years is a long time to wait, though. I could get drafted, or who knows what."

"Since Mary said she wants to talk to me, tell her I'll be home tonight." Trish stood, scooped up her purse and raincoat, and watched a frown shadow Otilio's face.

"She'll know I saw you."

Trish smiled. "Yep. Good luck."

TRISH FINISHED HER supper in front of the TV and kicked off her shoes. She sorted through a few bills and got up to answer the phone. It was Mary.

"Hi. I was expecting your call. Yeah, well I didn't mind. He means well."

Mary ticked off the pros and cons of marrying Otilio, and

Trish realized there was no way Mary would give up finishing her education. Otilio's parents had invited Mary to stay with them until her graduation and while Otilio found a place close to Hackensack.

"Why can't you two get married and live closer to Newark so you can get to class by bus?"

"He needs to be available in case they call him to cover a story at night, and the buses don't run often at night or on weekends. Even with his salary, we couldn't afford a car."

"Really? Fifty-five hundred a year is all? That's pretty shitty for a college graduate, isn't it?"

"I'll be making even less when I get a teaching job."

"Glad I wasn't smart enough to consider college. I do okay with tips, and I didn't have to bust my ass studying and end up drowning in debt when I got done." Trish thought of the black bag.

A COUPLE OF days after her conversation with Mary, Trish and Gabby had a day off. Trish made French toast and real coffee and they ate a leisurely breakfast after sleeping in.

"Do you think Mary and Otilio are too young to get married?" Trish asked, and then answered her own question. "They're pretty mature, I think, and he's getting a good job after graduation."

"In Puerto Rico, lots of girls get married at fifteen and sixteen. He's twenty-two and she's twenty, right? Not so young. I think they're a cute couple."

"Yeah, they are. Mary told me it's a problem because he has to live in Hackensack for his job and they can't afford a car. She'd have to take the bus for an hour and a half to get to her classes. She's not sure she could do that twice a day. If they could afford a car, they could live closer to Newark."

"Why can't they get a car? He'll be working."

Trish told Gabby what Otilio's salary would be.

"You shitting me? That's all?"

Trish nodded. "I think Mary wants to hold off getting married until she gets her degree, but he's worried he might get drafted or something if they wait."

"They're crazy to wait. Two years is a long time. They might as well be happy while they can. Besides, where would Mary live? She has no money for an apartment. You weren't thinking of inviting her to live here, were you?" Gabby's tone changed with her last question, so Trish answered quickly.

"No, of course not. His parents said she could stay there. Besides, we're moving soon."

The furrows on Gabby's brow smoothed out. "What's a used car cost?" she asked.

"What happened to your red Caddy?"

"Not for me."

"I have no idea. I could ask Rosalie. Her husband would know. Do you think we should give them money for a car?"

"Well, we have all that money. If it makes it possible for them to get married and lets Mary finish college, sure. It might be a good thing to do. Don't you think so?"

Trish got up and went over to Gabby's chair, put her arms around her neck, and kissed the top of her head. Gabby reached her hand up and took hold of Trish's arm.

"Does this mean you can be persuaded?"

"I could be. What'd you have in mind?"

"I'm thinking we should make sure the coffee pot's off and continue this discussion in the bedroom."

Gabby pulled her chair out, taking care not to catch the fraying edge of the rug. As she got up, Trish took a couple of steps back so she could see the stove.

"Coffee's off," she reported. She took Gabby's hand and led her along the hallway to the bedroom. When they reached the bedroom, Trish stopped. "It's awfully nice of you to want to help Mary. Thanks."

"You would do the same if it was my sister."

"Are you suggesting helping them because he's Puerto Rican," Trish teased, "or because she's my sister?"

"Maybe a little of both," Gabby answered. "What should we tell Mary about where we got the money to give them?"

Trish put her hand to her forehead and stared ahead. "I feel another lie coming on. Let's tell her we got lucky with the ponies."

"You think she'll buy it?"

"Why wouldn't she? Besides, it's a gift, so why should she question it? We'll say it's an early wedding gift."

"Let's not say an amount. Otilio can price used cars and tell us how much they need."

Trish pulled Gabby down on top of her and reached for the zipper on her slacks. Gabby kicked off her loafers and slipped her tongue into Trish's mouth.

Chapter Eighteen

"WHAT'S WRONG?" GABBY groaned, in the deepest part of a frosty night. "Why are you getting up?"

"It's nothing. Go back to sleep."

Trish grabbed the atlas on her way to the living room. She knew the New York page by heart. The puzzling church dream had occurred more often during the past few weeks and, for the first time, it felt like the pieces might fall into place.

"Please remember me the way you knew me," Mr. C's letter said. Salvatore Centimiglia...San Salvador...Holy Spirit...If the painting of San Salvador and the stained glass window with the Holy Spirit are near each other, that's where he wants me to look. But what about Tredita? Maybe he tossed that into the mix to confuse somebody who might have gotten hold of his letter. Trish knew she had to go back.

She was so wired she knew sleep was out of the question. She poured a glass of milk into a saucepan and heated it over a low flame. She sipped the warm milk and tried to stop thinking about Gloversville. Much as Trish itched to get back there, she was not about to chance it in midwinter. She'd have to wait until March or April.

Unwilling to risk an eruption if she brought it up to Gabby, she kept it to herself. In a personal bargain, she promised that if the painting was on the opposite side of the church from the stained glass window, she'd give up the chase.

For a few weeks, the dream occurred less frequently, and Trish took advantage of being able to stay asleep until the alarm clock went off. She read in *Reader's Digest* that applying wet tea bags would reduce swelling and had gone through a couple of boxes in the last month. She stared at her image in the bathroom mirror and tried to convince herself that the pillows under her eyes were shrinking.

TRISH SAID ONE morning over toast and Sanka, "You know,

I never said anything to you, but when we went searching for the pot of gold in Gloversville, I thought how nice it would be to set up a kind of charity to help people who need a break."

"Really, babe? I thought of doing something like that, too. I admit, I was more focused on covering our asses in case the money turned out to be stolen, though. Except for bending my elbow too many times, I really tried not to weird you out."

"Me, too. When we were in Cape May, I was sure the cops were gonna nab us when we started spending Mr. C's money. When nobody did, I wanted to believe it wasn't stolen. I wonder where he got that kind of money. He sure as hell didn't earn it working at the post office."

"No point worrying about it. We'll never know. If it was stolen from a bank, they have insurance. Trust me. Banks don't lose money."

"Speaking of banks, do we have to do anything about those traveler's checks? I mean, do they expire? Wouldn't it be a bitch if by the time we're ready to spend them, they're worthless? And what about the money orders? Do we need to deposit them in the bank?"

"Nah, we're good. They don't expire. I checked."

LATER THAT WEEK when Mary and Otilio visited, Trish and Gabby could hardly contain their excitement until dessert.

"Okay, you lovebirds, we have something serious to discuss with you." Trish explained their idea about an early wedding gift.

"Hey, will somebody please say something? I feel like we stepped in dog shit and brought it in on the rug." Gabby said.

Otilio cleared his throat a few times. "You want to buy us a car?"

"Yeah. If you had a car, you could live closer to Newark and still get to Hackensack to cover stories at night and on weekends if something happened. Mary would have a shorter bus ride to Rutgers, and you guys wouldn't have to put off getting married. Doesn't that solve your problem?"

At first, Mary sat like a statue. Then she spoke. "I, uh, I, um, know we shouldn't look a gift horse in the mouth, but where will you get that kind of money? Maybe I should forget teaching and get a job waitressing."

Their collective laughter broke some of the tension. Trish said, "If you promise not to tell anyone..." Mary and Otilio nodded. "We have a friend who's a bookie, and we give him a few bucks from time to time when he gets a hot tip. About a year ago, we hit a long lucky streak and we saved our winnings."

"Then you should do something nice for yourselves," Mary said.

"I'm not sure I can explain this," Trish said, and cleared her throat. "Having you back in my life has brought me a kind of happiness I never expected..."

"What am I, chopped meat?" Gabby demanded.

"That's chopped liver, and you're not either one. I'm very happy with you, okay?" Trish touched Gabby's arm.

Trish turned back to Mary and continued. "You will never know how rotten I felt when our parents turned you kids against me. Eventually, I wrote it off because I couldn't do anything about it. Then you showed up at the library that day, and spending time with you opened a part of my heart I thought was dead." She took Mary's hand and kissed it.

Gabby sniffed and Otilio coughed.

Trish turned to Otilio. "If my sister loves you enough to marry you, we want to do this thing. You're right. Two years is a long time, and if you get drafted, we want you to have a wife waiting for you at home. I learned losing time with people you love is stupid. Let us keep you from that kind of pain."

Gabby croaked, "Jesus Christ, Trish, my dinner is in my throat." She left the table and returned with a box of tissues.

"So, is it settled? You'll go shopping for a used car?"

"And set a wedding date?" Otilio added. He jumped up and moved to Mary's seat. On one knee, he took her hand and said, "Mary Mulkern, I want to spend the rest of my life with you. Will you marry me?"

"If you're sure you want me and not a car," Mary answered.

Otilio got to his feet. "Is that a yes?"

Mary nodded and Trish and Gabby applauded wildly. They all stood and fell on one another in a soggy heap.

"Excuse me," Gabby said. "I don't mean to be nosy, but isn't there supposed to be a ring?"

Otilio lowered his head and said softly, "I'm afraid it'll have to wait until I start my new job in June."

"I don't need a ring," Mary added.

Gabby left the room without explanation and returned in a minute with a small box. She held it out to Otilio. "My great-grandmother gave this to me right before she died. She said she hoped I'd wear it one day when I got married. I'm lending it to you until you buy one you like. Then, you can give it back to me in case I marry Trish."

"That means there's definitely no rush," Trish said.

Gabby handed the box to Otilio, and he opened it while Mary and Trish gathered closer for a look. The ring was gold with a red stone and two small diamonds on either side.

"It's a ruby," Gabby said, "and the two small ones are real diamonds. See the carving on the sides of the gold band? My great-grandfather was a jeweler, and he made it for my great-grandmother."

"Are you sure you want to lend this?" Otilio asked.

"See if it fits."

Mary held out her left hand and Otilio slipped the ring onto her fourth finger. It wiggled a bit. "It's beautiful, Gabby. I'll get a ring guard for it. I promise I'll take good care of it."

Looking at Gabby and Trish, Otilio said, "We can't thank you enough for this ring, which we will return as soon as we can, and for your love and the gift of a car. You'll be the first to know when we set the date."

Trish heard the huskiness in his voice. Mary walked to Trish and they hugged each other without speaking.

Then Mary said, "I never forgot you during those years. I remembered you as the big sister who took care of me and the others, and I knew in my heart I'd find you again one day. When we met at the bus stop downtown, I knew that even if you'd pushed me away, I wouldn't let you keep me out of your life. I'm not ballsy like you, but I can be tough when I need to be." Mary looked at Gabby and said, "You'll both be an important part of our family, always. Thank you so much." She reached for Gabby and Otilio for another four-way hug.

"We need to make tracks," Otilio said. "The bus stops here in half an hour."

"Maybe next time you come, you'll be able to drive home. You don't have to wait till the wedding to get the car. You'll need it to find an apartment. Call us when you know how much it will be," Trish said.

Gabby and Trish listened to the vestibule door open and close. They looked at one another.

"You are full of surprises, babe. Did your great-grandmother really give the ring to you?"

"What? You think I'd lie at a time like this?"

"Maybe, if you had a good reason. Did you?"

Gabby laughed. "You know me too well. I told a tiny fib. The ring was my great-grandmother's and she gave it to my mother. Mama wore it for many years until arthritis crippled her hands and she couldn't get it on anymore. She gave it to me when I went home last time, and said she hoped I'd find a nice guy and get married soon. I didn't tell you because I knew it would make you sad and mad. Each time I took it out of the drawer to look at it, it made me cry. We'll get it back one day and knowing it made them happy, maybe I won't cry over it anymore."

Chapter Nineteen

MRS. DONATO STOOD outside the building grinning at the first green crocus shoots poking their heads out of the ground. The contrast with the brackish puddles, left by melting snow in the window wells, offered hope to the tenants who trudged in and out on their way to and from humdrum jobs.

"You gonna stand and guard them till they come up?" Trish kidded her, after she'd spent hours sweeping away debris from the recent snow.

"Maybe. If those damned kids pull them up, I'll kill them."

Trish laughed the next night when she saw a small white-picket fence around the tiny plot of dirt. Good for you, Mrs. Donato, Trish thought. Better than murdering the neighborhood kids.

If the diner customers were a good barometer, everyone's mood seemed to lift with the milder weather. Some, who never talked to anyone, suddenly became chatty, a sure sign they'd become bored with their own company over the winter. Trish and the other girls benefitted from their newfound generosity.

TRISH AND GABBY'S site research pointed to a nice area in Pennsylvania that sounded so perfect, they planned to take off a couple of days to make a long weekend to check it out. It was a small town with pretty parks, and even had a diner. It was in the Pocono Mountains, but you could reach the airport in Philadelphia in two hours, a must-have for Gabby. It was far enough from Newark that they weren't likely to run into anybody they knew. They could buy a house, spend Mr. C's money however they wanted, and not have to lie to anybody about where the money came from.

Gabby took driving lessons so she could get a license. Trish didn't know how to drive either, but figured after Gabby got her license, she could teach her. She went along a couple of times while Gabby practiced parallel parking in Rosalie's car. All that shifting and clutching seemed awfully confusing. So many things to concentrate on. Trish wanted a car with an automatic shift. Those cars were more expensive, but they had the money, so she figured they might as well spare the aggravation.

Gabby passed the driving test on her second try, and they got Chinese take-out to celebrate. Otilio came by in the used four-door Ford sedan he'd bought with their wedding gift.

"Why don't you drive it?" he asked Gabby.

"Oh, God, no. It's too big."

Trish joked, "It's a tiny thing compared to the Caddy you want to get."

"All that parking made me think we should get something smaller. We'll see what kind of cars people in Stroudsburg drive. We don't want to stand out. I read that a lot of them are poor. They live in little houses because there are no apartment buildings."

"We'll check out the diner prices. That'll tell us plenty."

"They have an IGA supermarket. We'll check those prices, too."

Trish's pulse quickened whenever they talked about going to Stroudsburg. She had a good feeling about the place. They had tentative plans to visit in May. If they liked it, they'd contact a realtor. Trish preferred to live in town, but Gabby wanted to live a bit outside. She intended to plant a vegetable garden and dig a fishpond in the yard, exactly like the one on her family's property in San Juan, minus the palm trees. At least, that's what Trish thought until one evening.

Gabby read a gardening magazine and showed Trish photos of things she might put in their garden. "I was thinking," she said in a voice Trish recognized as trouble. "We could get some fake palm trees, like the ones on Broad Street in front of that fancy men's clothing store. They'd look great around the pond."

Trish hesitated and smiled. "Maybe we should put in a flock of pink flamingos, too...and some fake dinosaurs like at the beach...and a couple of giraffes..."

"Okay, okay, forget the palm trees."

IF THE WEATHER remained warm, Trish wanted to head back to Gloversville soon. Her good mood dipped when she considered how to tell Gabby. They'd gone several days without even a minor squabble. Why ruin the peace? But then, there was that dream...No point breaking the news to Gabby too soon. A week's notice would do. With Ignazzio out of the picture, Trish didn't anticipate any problems.

The early spring days galloped by and Trish chose a night when Gabby was exhausted. At eleven o'clock, she said, "I need to talk to you before we turn in."

"Sure. Wait till I brush my teeth. Gimme a minute. Can we talk in bed? I'm beat."

Trish had rehearsed what she planned to say and propped her head on one elbow. "I think it's time for Uncle Paddy to die. I need to go up to Gloversville one more time to check something out in the church." Trish sucked in her breath.

"Okay, fine." Gabby turned over and rearranged her pillow.

Trish spoke to the back of Gabby's head. "I thought I'd go up next Wednesday, spend the night, and return Thursday."

"Yeah, fine. Can I go to sleep now? I love you."

"Love you, too."

Trish stayed awake for hours trying to figure out what had just happened.

The next day, they worked the same shift and finished at three. They had salads in the back booth and Trish asked, "You aren't concerned about me going to Gloversville?"

"Yeah, well nobody's stalking you like the last time, so I'm not worried. You gotta do what you gotta do." Gabby stared into her plate as she spoke.

"I have to do this to make those dreams stop. I swear to God, if I can't solve the puzzle in Mr. C's letter, I'll quit and you'll never hear another word about it."

"You promise?"

Trish drew a cross over her heart.

"Good. Then we can concentrate on going to Stroudsburg to see if we want to live there."

Gabby began to laugh, softly at first and then the pitch rose to the level of hysteria. She clamped her hand over her mouth.

"Am I missing the joke? Let me in on it."

"I was going to let you sweat till you came back, but I can't keep quiet anymore."

"What the hell are you talking about?"

Gabby dabbed at her eyes with a napkin. "When you asked the boss if you could have two days off, he put it on the schedule in the office. I saw it right before he asked me if I was going to Saugerties with you to say goodbye to Uncle Paddy."

"You stinker. Why didn't you say something?"

"You left me hanging not telling me dear old Uncle Paddy had taken another turn for the worse. I nearly blew it when he asked me about it. Lucky for you, I'm a good actress. I told him I wasn't going this time, but I would probably need to go up with you in a few weeks to clear out his house and take care of things. That'll be our Stroudsburg trip."

Trish shook her head. "I swear I'll never be able to figure you out, babe. I can't predict what you'll do any more than I can predict whether the Yankees will win the pennant this year."

"I'm the one who hears you yell in your sleep about the Holy Spirit, or three fingers, or other wacky stuff. How could I not know it's been on your mind?"

"When did I start talking in my sleep?"

"You haven't stopped since we came back from the trip with Ignazzio, or Goldberg, or whatever his name is. I wasn't sure you remembered your dreams, so I didn't say anything."

"You know I would never go there without telling you, don't you?"

"I did wonder. We've told so many lies to people, I hoped you wouldn't start lying to me, too."

"So, you're not mad?"

"No, if it stops those dreams, it'll be worth the trip. Get it out of your system so we can get on with our plans." Trish squeezed Gabby's knee under the table.

THE WARM SUN and blue skies fueled Trish's hope that this would be a watershed day. She sat on the sunny side of the bus, hoping the tinted window would prevent sunburn but allow a tan. She read through most of the *Reader's Digest* by the time the bus reached Albany and wished Gabby was there to share the jokes. The Gloversville bus station seemed deserted except for one other person. Across the street, she spotted the lone taxi and asked the driver, "Can you take me to the Clover Leaf Motel?"

"You're lucky you didn't come last week. They got the mess from the fire cleaned up yesterday."

"Fire?"

"Yeah, they lost four rooms on the back side. They just reopened. Some idiot left a hot plate on in one of the rooms."

Trish got out and carried her suitcase. On her way to the motel office, she passed a pile of charred boards stacked in one of the parking spaces. She recognized the kid at the front desk from her last visit. He looked up and smiled.

"You need a room?" No, she thought. I came to see how you're doing, idiot.

"Are you alone, or is your friend with you?"

Maybe she underestimated the boy. He actually remembered there'd been two of them.

"Just me, this time. I'm here for one night."

"We had a fire."

"Really? Anybody get hurt?"

"We were lucky. I walked down the sidewalk to talk to the maid when I smelled something burning. I ran back, called the fire department, and unlocked the room where the smell was the strongest." He puffed out his chest and announced, "I pretty much had it out by the time they got here. Glad I was trained and knew not to throw water on an electrical fire. It's also a good thing it wasn't near a window or the drapes would have gone up. Most of the damage was caused by the firemen hosing down the nearby rooms. Only thing that burnt up was a desk and chair, and there were burns on the carpet." He pulled out a copy of the local paper with his photo on the front page. "Not a bad picture, huh?"

"Congratulations. You're a regular hero."

TRISH STOPPED AT the diner for a snack and coffee, something to tide her over before walking the few blocks to the Church of the Holy Spirit. She studied the menu since she planned to go back and have an early supper, and maybe take something to her room for later if she wasn't too depressed to eat. Actually, if that happened, it would have been a first. There were only a couple of customers in the diner and one waitress. Trish sat at the counter and surveyed the cakes and pastries in the glass containers. She was happy to see they did their own baking.

"Honey, if you're not in a hurry, I've got a fresh pot of coffee on. It'll be a minute."

The waitress brought an over-sized cheese Danish and, minutes later, a steaming mug of coffee. Trish knew the routine of chatting up customers to ensure a decent tip, but she really didn't want to endure the third degree when the waitress asked if Trish was visiting someone in town. Trish figured if the waitress was experienced, and she seemed to be, she'd take the hint when Trish answered with a curt 'no.' Smart lady. She left Trish alone except to bring the check.

THE FEW BLOCKS to the church seemed longer than she remembered, but at least it wasn't icy and windy like the last time. When Trish approached the church, she saw black and purple draping over the door. "Damn, it's Lent," she muttered. She hoped the religious Catholics had been to morning mass and gone home. She'd have felt uncomfortable taking flash pictures if people were around.

She moved her camera and shifted her purse to the side so she could use both hands to open the heavy wooden door. Once inside, she stopped as she was about to dip her fingers into the font containing holy water. Instead of genuflecting, Trish took a deep breath and entered the main part of the church. She waited while her eyes adjusted to the low light.

Her heart pounded as she walked around to the right side of the church, toward the window with the Holy Spirit. All of the statues were draped in the same black and purple cloths. She let out an audible gasp as she approached the window with the dove, and observed the painting of San Salvador hanging almost squarely beneath it on the stone wall. She removed a flash bulb from her purse and inserted it into the camera. Looking around to be sure there was nobody in the church, she stepped back into the pew to get the painting and the window in one shot. She held her breath, snapped the photo and frowned when the flashbulb lit up the entire section of wall.

"Damn!" she exclaimed, when she tried to remove the hot flashbulb. She put her burned finger in her mouth. Within minutes, the bulb cooled and she took it out and replaced it with a fresh one. To be safe, she took a second photo and hoped both would come out okay. It would be at least a week before she could retrieve them from the drug store.

Trish slid closer to the end of the pew to get a better look at the window. Her eyes focused on the dove's feet, and she clamped her hand over her mouth when she noticed each foot had three toes. "Holy shit. Tredita, just like my dream."

She retrieved a third flashbulb, put it in the camera, and took a closer shot of the bird's feet. No sooner had she taken the third picture, a priest entered the church from a side door and approached her. He was years younger than Father Rocco.

"Hello, I'm Father D'Alessio. Did you take a flash picture? Or are we having miraculous lightning in the middle of a sunny day?"

Trish saw him glance at the bubbled, browned flashbulb in the camera. "Yes, Father. I took a photo of this beautiful window. I've never seen another like it. Did I do something wrong?"

"This being Lent, I'd rather you not take any more photos. It might disturb people who are praying."

Since he was nice about it, Trish didn't point out that they were the only ones in the church. "Where's Father Rocco?"

"Who?"

"Father Rocco, the older priest who showed me around when I was here last time."

"I'm the only priest here, and I've been here for five years. When were you here?"

"It was in December."

"Oh, you must have been here while they were filming the documentary. I went away for a few days so they could use the church. They brought in an actor to host the program. That must be who you met. He wasn't a priest, though. What made you think so?"

"He offered to hear me and my friend's confessions a few times, and he was dressed like a priest. His robes were brown, Franciscan, I think."

"Oh, really? And did he hear your confession?"

"No, but he was really persistent."

"It sounds like somebody was playing a joke on you."

"Yeah, I guess."

"Well, feel free to stay as long as you like."

Trish listened carefully to the soft swish of the priest's black cassock as he walked the length of the church. She waited for a door to open and close before looking to see that he was gone. For the next fifteen to twenty minutes, Trish remained in the pew nearest the painting of San Salvador. From where she sat at the end, the wall wasn't more than five feet away, but the painting was at least ten feet off the ground. The lines from Mr. C's letter pounded in her head. "Please remember me the way you knew me, and stay close to the Holy Spirit."

There she was, as close to the Holy Spirit as she could get without a ladder, looking at the three-toed feet of the dove perched right above Mr. C's namesake. The money had to be there. She ran her hand along the irregular stones and remembered Mr. C telling her his father was a stone worker in Sicily. Could he have helped his son hide money in the church wall? If so, how could she get it?

Before leaving the church grounds, Trish opened the cemetery gate and wandered out to the place where the phony Father Rocco had said Mr. C was buried. The mound of dirt was gone. In its place stood a black granite headstone with Nicolo Catania's name and a beautiful etched violin. Next to the violin was a single rose and the scripted words, "An eye for an eye makes everyone blind." Making sure no one was around, Trish took a picture of the headstone.

TRISH RACED BACK to the motel and placed a collect call to Gabby. "Hi, babe. It's me. Sorry about the collect call. I had to call to tell you what I discovered at the church. There is no Father Rocco...No, he didn't die. He never existed." Trish related the conversation with the young priest. "Yeah, that's what I think, too. Bullshit and lots of it. What do you make of this?"

Gabby concluded that the private investigator had set the whole thing up, from the phony priest to the cock and bull story about Ignazzio being Mr. C's old friend. "Do you think they gave up after we couldn't find Tredita's grave?"

"I sure hope so. I don't think I was followed."

"You need to get the hell out of there. I wasn't worried before, but I am now."

"I'll be on the ten fifteen bus out of here tomorrow. I'm going to the diner to get something to eat and then back to my room. I'll be careful. I promise."

AFTER HANGING UP, Trish thought of something else. She walked to the office and hoped the young man was as dumb as she thought.

"Opening day is less than three weeks away," Trish said. "You a Yankees fan?"

"Me? Nah. Dodgers."

They chatted about their respective favorite players until she sensed she'd softened him up enough to ask, "You the manager here?"

"Yeah. I worked here part-time when I was in high school. After I graduated, they hired me as the day manager."

"I thought the woman who was here on my last visit was the manager."

His otherwise friendly face turned to stone. He shuffled papers and averted his eyes.

"Who was she?"

"I'm not supposed to discuss it," he said.

"What the hell is going on? Do I need to call the cops? I know she let somebody into my room after I left. Now, do you answer me, or do you want to tell it to the cops?"

"Look, miss," he pleaded, "I need this job. There aren't many good jobs in this town, and I don't want to get fired."

Trish read his nametag. "Listen, Dennis. I'm not trying to make a federal case out of this, and I don't want to make trouble for you, honey. The last thing I want is for you to get canned."

"Thanks for understanding."

"But this is literally a matter of someone's life and death." She smiled sweetly. "So, I need to know. I promise nobody will ever find out you talked."

He hesitated for only a moment before leaning over the counter and whispering, "They paid me fifty dollars to let her stay in the office. They didn't tell me what they were doing, but I figured it had something to do with you. She was working with the detective, the guy she let into your room a couple of times. That's all I know. I swear to God. After you left, she got into his car, and I never saw them again." He seemed on the verge of tears, and his voice trembled.

"Your secret is safe with me, Dennis. I won't say a word. I promise. Thanks." Trish walked slowly down the pavement to her room. "Score one for Gabby. Son of a bitch," she said to herself as she opened the door. Trish made a note to give Dennis a generous tip when she checked out in the morning. She couldn't match Greenberg's fifty, but she could try to make up for the grief she caused the kid.

Chapter Twenty

TRISH WAS PACKED and ready to leave the Clover Leaf Motel at eight the next morning. Since it was early, she took a taxi to the diner for breakfast. She read the local paper to kill time and asked the manager to call a cab at ten o'clock. When she arrived at the station, the bus sat empty. The driver picked up her suitcase and put it in the overhead rack. Trish sighed when the bus door closed. For a small town, Gloversville sure had the ability to raise her blood pressure. On the one hand, she wished never to see it again, but on the other, she was convinced that Mr. C's money lay hidden in the church wall.

During the boring trip down the New York Thruway, Trish visualized Mr. C's tombstone with its inscribed quote. She mused how he must have borne a heavy burden not being able to see his family for all those years. How sad. He sure hid it well, though. He always seemed so at peace with the world.

The hum of the bus and her heavy thinking wore Trish out and she dozed, waking up shortly before the bus pulled to the curb at Penn Station. Gray skies and drizzle notwithstanding, Newark was a welcome sight.

Trish carried her suitcase the few blocks to where she could catch her bus, pausing periodically to rest and massage her fingers. Thirty minutes later, the number thirteen bus stopped across the street from Albert's Candy Store just as Gabby walked in. Usually, Trish avoided the place because of an overwhelming magnetic force that always seemed to suck her over to the fountain to order a hot fudge sundae. Maybe with Gabby in there, she'd be safe.

She stepped in line behind Gabby, who was paying for a newspaper. "I'm home," she whispered loud enough for only Gabby to hear.

Gabby turned swiftly. "God, you scared me." She waved the newspaper at Trish. "I wanted to check the movies. You wanna go tonight?"

Trish waited until they left the store. "Movies? I was away.

Didn't you miss me?"

"You called me last night. How much time did I have to miss you?"

"Humph, I guess the honeymoon is over."

Gabby wasted no time once they reached their apartment. She towed Trish into the bedroom and whispered sexy things while she unbuttoned Trish's jacket and reached for the top button on her slacks.

"Don't you think we should lock the door?"

"Ugh, you're so practical." Gabby dropped the deadbolt and secured the chains.

Usually, it takes no time for Gabby to raise Trish's temperature. "What's the matter? You've been up to the far North and it froze your ass?"

"Don't give up so easily. I'm just really tired."

After some one-sided lovemaking, Gabby gave up and they both napped. Trish awoke first and tried to get out of bed quietly, but Gabby grabbed her arm.

"Where you going?"

"I need food. If I don't eat something, I'm gonna faint. You used up the little fuel I had."

RUMMAGING THROUGH THE refrigerator, Trish stopped suddenly when she saw a bottle of Corona beer in the door compartment. Oh no, she thought. Where did the rest of the six-pack go? Trish went back to the bedroom and coughed a couple of times to get Gabby's attention. Gabby turned over and saw the bottle in Trish's hand.

"It's not what you think. Since you were away, Otilio and Mary stopped by last night to keep me company. They thought I might be lonely. Otilio brought a six-pack, and they each had one. I convinced them to take the rest of the bottles with them but, after they were gone, I found one left in the fridge."

"Maybe you need to start telling people you don't drink alcohol, babe."

"Is that all you can say? How about being proud of me for not drinking it? That's the first time there's been alcohol in the house since I went on the wagon."

"Of course I'm proud of you. Was it hard?"

"To be honest, I've never liked beer. If it had been a bottle of Four Roses, I'm not sure what I would have done. I told that at the AA meeting I went to this morning."

Trish went back to scrounging for food. She found boiled ham that was dark around the edges. Since she couldn't remember when she'd bought it, she tossed it in the garbage. That's when she noticed two empty beer bottles. Surely, if Gabby had snuck alcohol, Trish was certain she'd have emptied the garbage.

Gabby padded into the dinette while Trish ate a half of a peanut butter and jelly sandwich and washed it down with milk.

"Neither of us has to work tonight. Want Chinese? I'll go pick it up. I have to drop my film at the drugstore, anyway."

They studied the takeout menu and Trish wrote down their choices. She put on the clothes she'd dropped on the bedroom floor, sniffed her armpits, splashed water on her face and left.

LATER THAT WEEK, Trish rushed from the bus stop to the drugstore a few minutes before its six o'clock closing time. The druggist was at the door as she reached for the handle. He waved her away holding up the 'CLOSED' sign he was about to hang on the door. Trish pointed to her watch and yelled, "Please, I won't take long."

"Okay," he said, opening the door. "What do you need?"

"My name is Mulkern. Did my pictures come in?"

"This is what was so important?" the druggist growled, as he walked behind the counter and sorted through a stack of envelopes.

"It's from my uncle's funeral," Trish said sweetly, trying to make him feel like a louse.

As soon as she got into the apartment she took the photos out. They weren't great, but they were good enough to show the details of what she had seen in the church and cemetery. Gabby brought their plates to the table and they talked over supper about what their next move would be. Gabby insisted Trish was not to go back to Gloversville without her.

"I think you're right," Gabby said, between bites after seeing the photos. "The money has to be in the wall. There's no other place it could be, unless..."

Gabby bit off another piece of chicken, and Trish watched as the sauce dribbled down her chin. With perfect timing, Trish caught the dribble with a napkin before it dripped onto the table.

"Unless what?"

"Unless he stashed it behind the picture. Did you look?"

"Shit, no." Trish smacked herself on the forehead, a habit she'd picked up from Mr. C. "It never occurred to me to check. I was so sure it was inside the wall. I couldn't have reached it, anyway."

Shifting gears, Gabby asked, "So, when can we go look for a house?"

"In Gloversville?"

"No, Stroudsburg."

"You're jumping way ahead of me," Trish said. "We're going to check the place out and see if we'd like to live there, right? Now you're talking about finding a house?"

"If we spend a few days in town, we should know if we want to live there. Then, if so, we can see a real estate person about finding a house."

"What if we don't like the town?"

"You'll have to invent another relative to kill off, so we can go to another funeral. Anyway, I have a feeling about Stroudsburg. It's a good feeling, and you always said you can trust my ESP."

"I admit, you're usually right. But let's give it a good look before we decide. I don't want to buy a house and then find out we hate the place."

Gabby nodded agreement. "Should we drive there?"

"In what?"

"I'm sure Otilio would lend us the car."

"You haven't even driven since you got your license."

"Maybe we should ask them if they want to go with us. They get a break week after next. We could have a good time while we get two more opinions about the place."

"And Otilio would do the driving. It might be fun, but we'd have to pay for everything. They don't have any money. I don't mind treating, but I'm not sure they'll let us."

"Well, ask them. We'd have to figure out sleeping arrangements, though. Remember, they're not married yet."

"We could get a room with two beds, one for you and me, and one for Mary. We can put Otilio on a cot. We'll be the chaperones."

"I'll tell the boss I need you to go with me to Saugerties to go through my uncle's stuff. He won't mind."

"Did you tell Mary we're going to be moving?"

"Umm...No. I thought I'd wait until we decide where we're going. I guess I have to tell her if we ask them to go with us to Stroudsburg, huh?"

"Of course you do."

Trish winced. "I think she'll be upset. We recently reconnected after so many years, and now I'm leaving her again. It'll be a shock. You want to tell her?"

"Hell, no. She's your sister."

Gabby's right, Trish thought, as she faced the mirror to remove her makeup. Why does everything involving family have to be so complicated?

To hear Gabby talk, family was something close to sacred. Her family nurtured her, and she only left them when economic necessity forced her to. Trish still feared she'd go back to them in a minute if she had enough money to help them live comfortably. Since inheriting Mr. C's money, the idea nagged at Trish constantly. If she thought they'd accept Gabby's relationship with her, she might have offered to help them get established in Newark, but she didn't want to add complications to their lives by having them nearby and being forced to act like she and Gabby were just good friends.

Trish and Gabby had several examples of what that looked like. They had friends who maintained a second bedroom so they could pretend they didn't sleep together when their families visited. Every time one of their relatives came for a meal, or even a short visit, they swept their apartment for any telltale signs they were a couple. They called it "sanitizing," which Trish hated. Their friends even put clothes in dresser drawers and closets in spare bedrooms so, if anybody snooped around, they'd be convinced one of them actually slept there. Gabby and Trish agreed they didn't want to live that way. It was bad enough they had to be careful at work, but that wasn't something they could control. They needed to keep their diner jobs, at least for a little while longer.

TRISH CALLED MARY the next time she had an evening off.

"Is this a good time to talk? I need to tell you something, and I think you might not be thrilled to hear it. No, we're both fine. Gabby and I are looking for a place to move to, someplace far from here, like maybe Pennsylvania."

"What? Why? Are you in trouble?"

"No, we're fine. It's a long story, and I can't get into it right now. We want to go to Pennsylvania to check out a place there. We'd like you and Otilio to come with us. We could make a little vacation of it. We'd pay for gas, motel, and meals if Otilio agrees to drive. I know you both have off for spring break soon."

"I don't have to go see any places in Pennsylvania. I hate them already."

"I didn't even tell you the name of the town."

"How far is it?"

"About a three-hour drive, and it's supposed to be a pretty area in the Pocono Mountains.

Trish heard Mary sniffle. "Are you okay, honey?"

"I just found you. Why do you have to move?"

"Like I said, it's complicated, but I promise I'll tell you on the way to Pennsylvania. Will you go with us? We really want you guys to help us make a decision about the town."

"Oh, great. Now I have to be an accomplice to help you run out of my life again?"

"Come on, Mary. That's a little over the top, don't you think? We could still talk on the phone, and you and Otilio can drive up and visit for weekends. Besides, you're going to be a bride living in a new apartment. You'll meet lots of new people, and make friends when you're not in class or studying."

"Wait a sec. Otilio just walked in and wants to know who died. Hang on a minute..."

"So, will you ask him about going with us?"

"Do you have dates in mind?"

"We can work it out after you talk to him. We can go any time during your break. I need to give our boss a couple days' notice, though."

Gabby appeared in the kitchen as Trish hung up the phone. "Well, are they coming with us?"

Trish exhaled. "Mary's very upset but she asked about dates, so maybe. She didn't argue about us paying for everything, but I don't know how Otilio will feel about it. Guys are funny about stuff like that."

"He took the money for the car and didn't squawk about borrowing the ring. He'll probably see it like they're doing us a favor. Besides, I'm sure he'll be relieved that we're not asking to borrow the car. At least if he drives, we have a chance of getting to Stroudsburg alive."

A FEW DAYS later, Gabby answered the phone. "It's Mary," she said, and covered the mouthpiece with her hand. "She's crying."

Assuming Mary was still upset about their moving plans, Trish took the phone. "Mary? Are you okay?"

Mary wailed, "I need my big sister." She cried for several seconds before asking, "Can you meet me somewhere so we can talk?"

"Where do you want to meet? I'm working till eleven tonight, and I only have a couple hours before I have to go in."

"That's not going to work."

"Can you tell me on the phone?"

Between bouts of crying, Mary described what she called the worst day of her life.

"Otilio and I went to a movie last night, which is something we might do maybe twice a year, if we're lucky. Who do you think we ran into?"

"I have no idea."

"Remember I told you about robbing that store when I was a kid, and the girl who did it with me? We were standing in the popcorn line and she walked right over. I recognized her immediately and nearly croaked."

"Oh, no."

"I introduced Otilio as my fiancé, figuring she'd have enough sense not to say anything stupid. Boy, was I wrong. She looked right at him and said how we went way back and that we'd gotten arrested together. She laughed while I stared daggers at her."

"I hope you told him she was a jokester, and that she said it to be funny."

"I wish I was as fast on my feet as you. As soon as she walked away, he asked what that was all about. Not wanting to talk about it in the theater, I said I'd tell him later. He took my hand

and steered me out of the theater."

"He didn't hit you, did he?"

"I almost wish he had. We sat in the car and I told him what happened. Being from a poor family, I thought he'd understand, but he got on his high horse and called me a thief and a liar."

Trish twirled the phone cord so tightly around her fingers it threatened to cut off the circulation.

"I was afraid he was going to say he didn't want to marry me, but the whole way home, he didn't say a word. I cried and begged him to understand that we needed the food, but he sat there staring ahead with his jaw clenched like he does when he's mad. When we got home, he went to his bedroom and I didn't see him for the rest of the night."

"You poor thing. Is this your first fight?"

"We've had arguments, but nothing like this. I saw him this morning, before he left for school. All he said was that we needed to talk when he got home. I left for class a few minutes later, and I swear I never heard a word the professor said. I just got home and picked up the phone to call you."

"Maybe Otilio will cool off today. Is he mad about what you did, or because you didn't tell him?"

"He said it shows a major flaw in my character. He thinks I should have told him about it when we started dating."

"Oh, give me a break. Didn't he ever do anything illegal? Maybe you should think seriously whether you want to be married to somebody so perfect." Though Mary couldn't see it, Trish spit out the words through clenched teeth.

"I think I hear the car pulling up. I don't want him to know I called you."

"If he loves you as much as I think he does, you'll work this out, honey. Call me tomorrow and let me know how it goes, okay?"

Mary whispered, "He's home. Yes, I'll call."

Since Gabby had only been listening to Trish's side of the conversation, Trish filled her in.

"It's his pride," Gabby concluded. "He's just pissed off because somebody knew something about Mary that he didn't know. Maybe he's had time to think about how he'd like to start taking the bus again."

"Huh?"

"No wedding, no car. If he breaks off with Mary, he can turn the keys over to her."

"I feel so bad for her. Of all the shit luck to run into that woman after all this time. You think she did it on purpose, telling him that?"

"Maybe she's got a rotten life and wants everybody else to have one, too. Where's Mary gonna go if he throws her out? Never mind. That's a stupid question. She'll come here."

"You mean it? You'd let her live with us?"

"Where else is she gonna go with no money and no job? She has to finish college so she can be a teacher."

Trish grabbed Gabby in a bear hug and was surprised when Gabby pulled away.

"And another thing. I'll take a bus to their place to get back the ring. While I'm there, I can pick up the car and Mary."

"Don't jump the gun. I think they'll work things out. Otilio's crazy about her. He's not stupid enough to throw away their chance at happiness."

"People have done dumber things. We'll see."

TWO DAYS LATER, Trish said, "If she doesn't call, I think my head's gonna explode. Even aspirin won't dull this headache. I called twice, and the younger kids answered. All I could get out of them was that Mary wasn't there. If he did something to her, I swear I'll kill him. I'm calling in sick tonight. Let's go over there."

"I'll tell the boss we can't come in tonight. We've both got the trots," Gabby said. "I'm sure we'll be better by tomorrow."

Trish and Gabby took a bus downtown and transferred to a second one. "This is the perfect time to go. He cooks for the kids, so they'll probably be home."

Standing in front of Otilio's house, Gabby saw the kids inside. "I don't see the car, but somebody has to be in there with them."

Trish rang the bell and a woman she guessed was Otilio's mother answered. "Hi, I'm Trish, Mary's sister. Is she here?"

Gabby chimed in speaking Spanish, hoping it might yield additional information. The woman invited them to come in and wait, but Gabby refused.

"She says they went out to eat and should be back soon. I told her there's a family crisis and it's very important that you speak to Mary. She promised to give her the message."

"Well, at least we know they're together. That's a good sign. Let's go home."

WALKING TOWARD THEIR building, Trish stopped in her tracks. "Isn't that their Ford?" She pointed to a parked car a few doors from their building.

They walked to the car, and Trish opened the door. "What are you guys doing here?"

Mary answered, "We thought we'd surprise you by showing up at the diner for supper, but we got the surprise when they said you were both out sick. We came over to see how you were."

"You don't look sick to me," Otilio said. "What's up?"

"We just came from your house. Your mother said you went out to eat, but we never thought you'd come to Scotty's. Did you eat?"

"No, we were worried about you. We've been sitting here for over an hour."

"Feel like Chinese?" Gabby asked.

"Sure. Hop in."

Over supper, Mary explained that Otilio came to his senses and, in her words, "quit acting like the Pope."

"You're lucky that your father works in a restaurant. No matter how bad off your family is, at least he can always bring home food. All our father brought home was booze, and that's not recommended for growing children."

"Yeah, I know. After our fight, I thought about that. I used to assume the food he brought home was leftovers, but I asked him about it one time and he said he deliberately cooked too much so he could bring food home. That was before my mother got a job and helped out. He said it made up for the lousy salary he got."

"So, he stole food to feed his family, just like Mary," Gabby said.

"Exactly." Otilio put his arm around Mary's shoulders. "It's one of the things I love about her. She always puts others ahead of herself. How could I stay mad?"

"We've agreed not to keep secrets from each other from now on," Mary said.

Trish and Gabby smiled at each other then at Mary and Otilio. "That's a good goal," Trish said, knowing it would likely be as impossible for them to achieve as it was for her and Gabby.

"I CAN'T BELIEVE the amount of luggage you're taking for a weekend," Otilio complained, as he packed the trunk.

Trish stood next to him and tucked a ten dollar bill into his pocket. "For gas."

Otilio looked away, but she heard him say, "Next time we go on a vacation together, I'll be working."

"Think of it this way. You're saving our lives. Can you picture Gabby driving so far without hitting something?"

He smiled and grunted as he struggled to fit the suitcases in the trunk. Finally, after some persistent rearranging, he slammed it closed. They piled into the car and Otilio drove to the highway leading north.

"So," Mary said, "tell us why you have to move."

"All right. You know Gabby and I don't make much money at the diner. We had this friend, Mr. C, an elderly neighbor in our building. He was alone and had no family or friends, and we kind of looked after him. We got groceries for him and helped out. When he died last year, he left a note telling me to get this bag from his closet and keep what was in it. It was full of money, several thousand dollars. That's where we got the money we gave you to buy this car, and that's why we're retiring and moving someplace nicer than Newark. So, now you know the story."

"But why do you have to go so far? You could get a nice place in Newark."

Gabby scrunched her face like a prune. "You serious? I want to be somewhere with trees and clean air. I haven't breathed right since I left San Juan. Trish won't move to Puerto Rico, so we're looking for someplace closer. That way, you guys can come visit."

Trish noticed Otilio place his hand on Mary's thigh. When she saw him raise his eyebrows in the rearview mirror, she was grateful that Mary got the message. The rest of the ride to Stroudsburg was quiet, except for the static on the radio each time Mary tried to get a station with clear reception.

The landscape in northern New Jersey was a far cry from Newark. Pine trees lined the sides of the road. As the car neared the large gap drilled down by the Delaware River, Gabby said, "Boy, are we still in New Jersey? This is beautiful."

"I heard it was nice up here," Trish replied. "Rosalie's husband drives her up here once in a while, and she told me about it."

Otilio pulled into a rest stop and they all stretched their legs. "Ooh, smell this," Trish said, and held up a low-hanging branch for all of them to sniff. "It reminds me of those little log cabins with incense we had as kids. Just leave me here. I could overdose on the scent."

The clerk at the information desk told them they were about to cross the river into Pennsylvania. "You're about five miles from Stroudsburg. Make sure you eat the chicken and dumplings at the Lady Stroud Diner," he called, as they headed for the exit.

"Look at that old guy. He's a dead ringer for Santa Claus," Otilio said, as they passed the Stroudsburg Welding Company. He slowed to twenty miles an hour and asked, "Are razors illegal here?"

as they passed several men in overalls with long beards.

"They're Amish," Trish said.

"Is everyone here named Yoder?" Mary asked, as they passed Yoder's Hardware, Yoder's Farm Supply, and Yoder's Cheese Shoppe in quick succession.

Trish shared what she could remember about the early settlers of the area until Mary shouted, "There's the diner."

"SURE IS DIFFERENT from Scotty's," Trish remarked, as they read their menus. "My God, look how cheap this stuff is."

Everything sailing past on steaming plates looked great. One platter in particular caught Gabby's eye. She'd always loved Swanson's frozen potpies, but these looked homemade. She and Mary ordered chicken potpies while Otilio got the meatloaf blue plate special, and Trish tried the chicken and dumplings.

Trish and Gabby had the muscles to prove how big the portions at Scotty's were, but the servings here were too huge even for Otilio's appetite.

"I need to walk off some of this food," Trish said. "I'll burst if I sit so soon."

They strolled through the six-block downtown, wandering in

and out of stores. Trish stopped at a realty office and perused the photos of houses in the window. "Should we go in?" she asked Gabby.

Gabby laughed. "Maybe we should go to our motel first and look around some more. You're not ready to make a decision, are you?"

Trish smiled at her impulsiveness. "I guess not."

THE SHORT VACATION in Stroudsburg made the decision to relocate easier than they'd expected. It was much less stressful than determining whether or not they should attempt to claim the money Trish was sure lay behind the painting in the Gloversville church.

Over several weeks following the trip to Pennsylvania, Gabby alternately stormed through the apartment convinced that Mr. C's money was loot from a bank heist and trying to persuade herself and Trish that there was some other explanation.

Trish was not ready to believe their friend had robbed a bank, even to save the lives of his parents and brothers. But she knew far more about Mr. C's past than Gabby did.

"If we went there and found the money, we could always turn it over to the cops or the bank," Trish offered, as an inducement to get Gabby to go back to the church.

"What if they're watching the church? You wanna risk getting arrested? I wish we knew who hired Ignazzio. If it was the bank, I bet they gave up after he saw we didn't know anything. Or maybe they went and found the money and don't need us anymore.

"Hmm, never thought of that."

Chapter Twenty-one

"IS EVERYTHING ALL right?" Rosalie asked Trish one night soon after she and Gabby had returned from the latest deathbed visit to Uncle Paddy. "You've been unusually quiet."

"I'm worried about my uncle. How many times can he spring back from death's door? Every time the doctors say this is the end, he makes liars out of them."

"He must not be ready to go. You hear stories all the time about people who hang on for months, when everybody says they don't know what's keeping them alive."

Two of the girls who overheard their conversation volunteered stories about relatives who cheated death for years. Trish hoped their relatives were more real than Uncle Paddy.

"I'D LOVE TO tell Rosalie why we're moving," Trish said to Gabby that night.

"If you do, she'll know you've been lying for the past year. You want her to remember you that way?"

"No. I swear if we ever buy a house and move to Strouds-burg, I'll never lie again. I've had more headaches in the last six months than in my whole life."

Gabby tweaked the rabbit ears for a few minutes until the picture on the TV screen was only slightly snowy. At the end of Dragnet, Sergeant Friday solved the robbery, as usual, and in his serious way told his partner, "There are two kinds of people in this world; those who do the right thing when they think nobody's watching, and those who do the right thing only when they think somebody's watching."

"I think I'm the second kind," Gabby said, as they got into bed. "How about you?"

"Depends," Trish replied. "There are some things I'd never do, even if I thought I could get away with it, like murder. I wouldn't be able to kill somebody. Would you?"

"I could if somebody did something awful to me or to you. Say, if somebody was gonna rape you and I had a gun, I'm sure I'd shoot him without thinking twice. I'd worry about going to jail later."

"Well, if you put it that way, I might do it to protect you, too."

Trish snuggled close to Gabby and yawned, blowing hot air onto Gabby's neck.

"What about Mr. C's money?" Gabby asked.

"It's got to be in that church," Trish said. "You think so, too, right?"

"Maybe, but I'm not so greedy I want to risk going to jail. We have plenty of money. Why take the chance? I still can't figure out why that sweet old man had to go to all of this trouble to leave us this money. Why couldn't he just put it in a bank account like everybody else does?"

Trish sat on the edge of the bed and put the lamp on. "It's not so simple, babe. Remember the vendetta Mr. C mentioned in his note?"

"Yeah, you said he beat up some kid in Sicily or something..."

"Umm, he did more than that. After he realized he couldn't play violin anymore, he found the kid who broke his arm and...don't freak out on me...he cut off two fingers on the kid's hand, the same two Mr. C had no feeling in after the surgeon tried to fix his arm."

"If this is your idea of a joke, it's not funny. Don't scare me, Trish. Mr. C would never do something like that."

"I was shocked, too, when he told me. It's true. I thought maybe that's why he left Sicily so the cops wouldn't lock him up, but he said everyone there knew he had to do it, to settle the score."

"Jesus, Maria y Jose. What kind of people are they?"

"After his family moved to New York, the two brothers of the kid whose fingers Mr. C cut off came to settle the score. I know how upset you get about stuff like this, so I told you it was just crazy guy shit, but Mr. C told me they were serious about killing his family unless he agreed to rob a bank with them. That's why it's important that his parents and his brothers didn't all die at the same time. I think it means he might have robbed the bank to save them. It's all part of that vendetta shit."

Gabby jumped out of bed and began pacing around the apartment. "I need a cigarette," she said.

"You don't smoke."

"It's that or a drink!"

Trish reached for Gabby's arm and pulled her down next to her on the bed. "This is why I didn't tell you. You get so crazy. This all happened a long time ago. Maybe they just tried to scare Mr. C and when he left town, they gave up. Those brothers probably went back to Sicily, or maybe they're dead by now. They would have been older than Mr. C."

"Maybe. If they were still around, we'd probably be dead. So that's why Mr. C changed his name. He did it to protect his family."

"I'm betting everybody connected with this thing is dead now, so it's probably safe to try to find the money. I wouldn't feel right if we didn't at least try. Mr. C really wanted us to have it."

"Okay, Sherlock, so how do we get the money out of the wall without the priest seeing us?"

"Remember how the priest fell for Ignazzio's scheme about doing a documentary on the church? If he bought it once, he'll be an easy mark for a second one."

"So, what are you gonna do, blow the wall out while he's away?"

"C'mon, babe, give me a little credit. I've got a plan."

"Oh, this should be good." Gabby lay back down and put her hands behind her head. "Go ahead."

"Okay, this is how we'll do it. We arrange for this film company to use the church for a few days to shoot a movie about the art. We hire somebody to bring in ladders and equipment and put a 'Closed for Repairs' sign on the door. Then we take down the painting and loosen the stone, or crack the safe, or whatever's back there."

"Who you gonna get to remove a stone or crack a safe?"

"The goombahs."

"What goombahs?"

"The ones who come to the diner all the time. We'll offer them money. We know they can keep their mouths shut. What do you think?"

"All these years and I didn't know I was living with a criminal." Gabby shook her head. "A friggin criminal right in my own bed."

"Does that mean you won't do it?"

"You trying to test me to see if I'll start drinking again?"

"Of course not. It's a good plan. I'm sure it'll work."

"You're scaring me, Trish. What if the cops break the church door down and catch you? I wouldn't put it past the goombahs to shoot the cops. Then you'd be up on murder charges. It's not worth it. We have enough money. Please don't do this."

"We don't have to decide anything tonight. I'll think about what you said. Turn over." Trish slid into place behind Gabby. She kissed the nape of Gabby's neck and massaged her shoulders. Gabby fell asleep in minutes, but Trish couldn't turn off her mind. She knew Gabby had a good point about the goombahs. They were kind of crazy. She needed to talk to Rosalie about them.

"WHEN YOU TAKING your break?" Trish asked Rosalie at work the next day. "I got something I want to ask you. Let me know, and I'll take mine the same time."

"It's nice out. Let's go out back. I need some air." Rosalie opened the back door and Trish followed. "So, what's up?"

"You know the goombahs, right? You said they work for the same guy Sean does."

"Yeah, why? You need a reference?" Rosalie brayed at her joke.

"Would you trust them to do something for you?"

"Depends. I wouldn't hire them to babysit, but I'd trust them to do something that didn't involve cops or the FBI." Rosalie looked straight at Trish. "You know they're gangsters, right?"

"Yeah, yeah, I know. Do you think they can keep their mouths shut?"

"They're alive, ain't they? What are you thinking?"

"Do you feel safe around them?"

"Oh, sure. They're very respectful around women. Remember the time that drunk grabbed your ass and they stepped in? And I told you they threatened my old man if he hit me again. Are you up to something?"

"Nah. I have a friend who needs to hire somebody to take care of some punk who's bothering her. Nothing real serious, just to rough him up so he'll leave her alone."

"Oh yeah, I'd trust them to do that. Just tell your friend to be very clear that she doesn't want the punk killed. These guys play rough, and they only work for cash."

Chapter Twenty-two

"I'M A NERVOUS wreck," Mary said, as Otilio pulled away from the curb in front of Trish and Gabby's building. "For a while, I'd convinced myself you would never get up the nerve to move, but now we're actually going to see a house you picked out."

"Listen, little sister, if there's one thing we've got, it's nerve. We might come up a little short on smarts, but you gotta admit that between Gabby and me, we got a good pair." She reached for her crotch.

Otilio asked, "Pair? Pair of what?"

"Those things you got that are gonna make us aunts after you two get married."

Trish saw Otilio's flushed face in the rearview mirror.

"We should have gone on a rainy day," Mary said. "Do you realize both times we've gone to Pennsylvania, it's been a beautiful day? Maybe you should see it in lousy weather."

"It won't make any difference. The day I rented our apartment it was gray and drizzly, and the place never looked any better on sunny days."

Gabby added, "It's an omen. I think this house was meant to be ours."

"You been having visions again?" Otilio asked.

Gabby closed her eyes and put her hand to her forehead. She said in a weird voice, "I see a two-bedroom house in a small town in our future."

They all laughed at her theatrics.

SUZANNE, THE REALTOR, came out of the office when they arrived. "Right on time," she said. "We can go in my car if you're tired of driving."

"No, I'm good," Otilio replied.

Trish and Gabby slid over to make room. Suzanne navigated,

and in five minutes they reached the house.

"Here we are. Are all of you coming in?"

"Sure. We want this to be a group decision," Trish answered.

The house was small, so it didn't take long for Suzanne to show all of the rooms. Trish had a good feeling about it and so did Gabby, but they searched Mary and Otilio's faces. Otilio did his guy thing and asked several questions, none of which Suzanne hadn't already answered the last time Trish and Gabby were there. She was polite and answered him as if she'd never been asked before. She explained the house was originally heated with coal, but the owners modernized it and put in oil heating. Trish had grown up in an apartment with a coal furnace and always hated the smell, so she was happy about that.

After Otilio ran out of questions, Suzanne said, "I'll step outside so you folks can talk."

"So, what do you think?" Trish asked Mary and Otilio.

Otilio jumped in. "You never pay the asking price. You have to negotiate."

"Did you ever buy a house?"

"I asked my father. Houses and cars, they always ask more than they expect you to pay."

"Suzanne said it costs $10,999. What should we say?"

"Offer nine thousand and let her counter with $9,500 or $10,000."

If Trish was honest, she'd admit she wanted to ask Otilio to handle the negotiating, but she didn't want him to think she and Gabby couldn't do it.

"The horse is running away with the cart, people," Gabby said.

They all stood for a moment. "You mean we're putting the cart before the horse?" Trish asked.

"Whatever it is." Turning to Mary and Otilio Gabby pressed, "You haven't said what you think of the house."

Otilio gestured for Mary to begin. She looked at Trish tearfully and then at Gabby.

"I hate to say it, but I love it. I think it's a perfect house for you. The yard is great, too. If you put a fence around it, you can have a dog and it'll have someplace to run. Otilio and I can help you take down the swing set, since I guess you won't need it."

"Maybe you should take it in case..."

Mary turned to Otilio. "What do you think?"

"I love swing sets."

Mary punched his arm. "Come on, be serious."

"Which one is our bedroom?"

"Woo hoo!" Gabby hooted. "See? I told you."

"Wait," Trish shouted. "I forgot something." She ran to each bathroom and flushed the toilets. "Everything's cool," she reported. "Let's tell Suzanne."

Expecting Mary and Otilio to love the house, Trish had cashed in traveler's checks and deposited the money into her checking account. Gabby and Trish went into Suzanne's office to talk about money while Otilio and Mary waited in a conference room.

"I'LL HAVE TO check with the sellers to see if they're willing to accept your offer," Suzanne replied to the nine thousand dollar figure. "I'll call you after I talk with them."

"Can't you call them now?" Gabby asked. "It could save us a trip back here."

"Well, we usually don't do it that way, but let me check."

Suzanne disappeared into another office and closed the door. When she returned, she was smiling. "Mr. Stroud, the owner of the agency, is a personal friend of the sellers, so he called Mr. Mueller." She stuck out her hands and said, "Congratulations. He accepted your offer."

For a moment, neither said anything. Suzanne left to fetch forms. Trish whispered to Gabby, "If I'd known it was so easy, I'd have offered less."

"We'll need a check for ten percent of the price," Suzanne said when she returned. "You can mail it to me."

"You won't take it now?" Trish asked. She quickly calculated what ten percent was.

"Oh no, it's fine. I thought..."

Trish waved off the rest of her comment and took out her checkbook. Gabby watched as she wrote out a check for nine hundred dollars. Suzanne took the check and returned with a receipt and more papers. Trish excused herself and went out to let Mary and Otilio know they might be a while.

"You saved us two thousand dollars," she said beaming.

"They accepted our offer."

"No kidding. Wait till I tell my father. What happens now?" Otilio said.

Mary got up and hugged her sister. "I promise I won't cry again. I'm so happy for you guys."

Trish was grateful that Mary didn't comment on her shaking.

"We have to go over a bunch of stuff. We might need another hour. You wanna go out and play tourists and come back in an hour? Maybe you can get some lunch."

"Want us to bring you sandwiches?"

"I'm not hungry, but Gabby might want one."

Trish took five dollars out of her wallet and handed it to Mary. Waving off Mary's protest, Trish reminded her they'd just saved two thousand dollars, thanks to Otilio.

Halfway through the paperwork, Trish had to use the rest room and saw Mary and Otilio heading up the walk with paper bags. "Maybe another twenty minutes," she called to them.

The Muellers had moved out three months earlier and were eager to close. Since it was a cash deal, the transaction was on the fast track. Suzanne said she'd call to tell Trish and Gabby when to return to Stroudsburg to take possession of the house. Gabby alternated chewing her cuticles and twirling her curls, while Trish's feet tapped out a rhythm under the table.

The ride home was quiet. Gabby devoured her sub while Trish barely gnawed on hers, deciding it was better not to force any food into her stomach.

When they were nearly home, Gabby said, "Let's get a dog."

"I never had one. What kind?"

"We had a black Lab in Puerto Rico. They're sweet. I think you'd like that kind."

Trish shrugged. "I guess so. A dog's a dog. You're in charge of walking and feeding it. Do they come house broken? I'm not cleaning up dog shit."

"Don't worry about it. I know what to do."

Mary dozed in the front seat until the car stopped. When she got out to say goodbye, she took Trish's hand. To everyone's great surprise, tears flooded Trish's eyes.

The sisters hugged and Trish whispered, "I love you." She realized it was the first time she'd said those words to anybody but Gabby in her entire adult life.

Chapter Twenty-three

"WHAT ARE YOU doing?" Trish asked Gabby as she sat poring over papers spread across the dinette table.

"I'm figuring how long our money will last."

"Did you subtract what we've already spent?"

"Yeah, I think I got everything. You can help. Count up how much money we have in traveler's checks and money orders. You kept all the checks and money orders in the black bag, right?"

"Of course. As soon as we converted the cash, I put all of it in the bag. I don't need to count them. I've been writing down how much we spent from Mr. C's money." Trish pulled out a slip of paper from her purse. "We have $94,150 left."

Gabby looked up from her calculations. "After we pay for the house, let's say we take half of the money and invest it. We could live on the rest of it for at least ten years. Figuring we'll make money on the part we invest, we should never have to work again."

"Look, babe, I don't know anything about investing. Can you lose money by investing it?"

"Sure. It's like gambling. That's why we'd only put half the money in investments."

"I don't know if I want to gamble away half of Mr. C's money. Suppose we lose it? Nix this investing idea. Let's put it in the bank once we move to Stroudsburg and let it earn interest. I heard that if you keep it in a bank, the government insures it in case the country goes broke. There are people who know about this stuff. We should go see somebody."

"Who? Somebody like Rosalie's husband?"

"Get outta here. No, I mean somebody legit who can give us good advice. I'm sure there's someone in Stroudsburg. We won't have to explain where we got the money. We can say I inherited it."

"What I'm saying is we don't need any more money."

"So you still think we shouldn't try to get the rest of Mr. C's money?"

"Right, and I hope I can make you see sense. It's too danger-
ous. You could end up in jail or dead. Please tell me you won't go
there anymore."

"I won't do anything till we talk it over. I have thought about
what you said. You raise some good points."

Trish knew if she was ever going to get the rest of Mr. C's
money, she'd have to do it without Gabby. The last thing she
wanted was for Gabby to start drinking again, so she began plot-
ting. A few days later, she told Gabby she needed some time
away alone with Mary before the move to Stroudsburg.

ONE NIGHT WHEN Trish worked the late shift and Gabby
wasn't around, she talked with the goombahs. "What makes you
think we'd do something illegal?" the taller one, Vincent, asked
after she'd outlined her plan.

"Who says anything is illegal?" Trish asked. "Do I look like
some kind of criminal?"

He looked at his friend, Carmine, or Little Carmine as Vincent called him, and said something in Italian. Little Carmine,
who must have weighed two hundred pounds from his waist to
his knees alone, shrugged and answered, "Why not?"

"I like you, Trish. You always been straight with us, no bullshit or nothing, so we'll help you out. I got one question, though.
Where's a dame like you come up with two grand? Not that I
don't trust you, but I gotta see the dough before we do the job."

"I'm hurt, Vincent. You think I'd cheat you?" Trish wished
she could force herself to cry.

"Nah, it's not that I don't trust you. I didn't mean no disrespect. It's the way we do business, is all."

"Well, I'm not used to paying for work until the job's done,"
she answered. "I didn't just get off the boat, boys."

More Italian talk between Vincent and Little Carmine. Trish
wished she'd taken Italian in school instead of bookkeeping.

"I'll tell you what. I like you boys, and I know you wouldn't
cheat a working girl like me. I'll give you a thousand up front and
the rest after you do the job."

Vincent looked at Little Carmine. "You got yourself some
partners."

Trish hated the thought of them possibly ripping her off for a grand, but the set of Vincent's jaw told her she couldn't negotiate anything better. They shook hands.

"When do you need us?" Little Carmine asked.

"I have some details I need to take care of first. You gonna be around for a few weeks?"

"Yeah, we ain't going nowhere." Vincent wrote a phone number on a napkin and gave it to her. "If you don't see us here, give me a call. Oh, and if a dame answers, hang up. My wife thinks every woman in Newark is after me." Little Carmine snorted and Vincent added, "I should be so lucky."

NOW ALL TRISH had to do was figure out how to get the priest out of the church for a couple of days. She hoped Little Carmine didn't suffer a major heart attack. She hadn't told the guys what was hidden in the church, just that it was something valuable that belonged to a good friend. They were no dummies. She was sure they figured out it was either money, or something worth a lot of money. She also hadn't told them they needed to dress like movie makers so nobody would get suspicious if they saw them go into the church with ladders. Trish had only seen them in silk suits and expensive ties, so it might not take much for them to look the part.

Chapter Twenty-four

"HELLO FATHER D'ALESSIO. My name is Genevieve Abbondante. I'm with Beatitude Film Group, an independent Christian film company, and we're interested in shooting a couple of scenes in your church. We know you've allowed others to film at Church of the Holy Spirit, and would like to talk about how we might arrange that for our company. We're especially interested in the art."

"Yes, we do have a magnificent art collection. Some of the paintings are written up in books about church art, but I guess you know that. When did you have in mind, Miss Abbondante?"

"Oh, we'll do it at your convenience, Father. Of course, we'll be happy to make a generous contribution to cover any utilities and inconvenience to you and your parishioners." Trish hoped that got his attention.

"Let me check our calendar. Is it okay if I call you in a few days?"

Trish reached over her shoulder and patted her back. Wow, she thought, that was easier than I expected. For the next few days every time she answered the phone, "Beatitude," people thought they had the wrong number. Trish made sure Gabby worked days that week. The phone rang one morning when Trish was home alone.

"IS THIS MISS Abbondante? This is Father D'Alessio from Holy Spirit. I checked our calendar, and the earliest I could let you use the church is next week. Would Thursday and Friday work?"

"I think so, Father. Let me take a quick look at our production schedule...Yes, we can do it then."

"Would you need to see the church before then?"

"Actually, we've already seen it. One of our location scouts visited several churches in your area, including Holy Spirit, and recommended it to us. We're doing a documentary about church art, and he was especially impressed with your stained glass windows and paintings."

"Oh, we're honored. We are blessed with a very beautiful church." He hesitated before saying, "You had mentioned a donation?"

"Of course. Our usual donation is a hundred dollars for each day."

"Oh, that's most generous. Thank you."

"Our director will plan to stop by to see you on Wednesday, and you can show him anything you consider off-limits. We want to respect church property. He'll bring the donation. You've had film crews in the church before, so I'm sure you understand that nobody can be there while we're shooting."

"Oh yes, I've already told the church secretary she can have those two days off, and I'm going to visit my mother in Connecticut."

"While we work, we usually put a sign on the door saying the church is closed for repairs. Okay?"

"Sure, good idea. You know how some people are. They all want to be movie stars. This way, they won't know what you're doing."

Got that right, Trish thought. Perfect.

"You need to wrap it up Friday, though. I'll have to get back into the church on Saturday to hear confessions."

"Of course, Father. We will be sure to take everything with us when we leave Friday." She smiled, picturing the bag of cash she expected to carry out.

TRISH CALLED VINCENT that night and was relieved when he answered. "Vincent, it's Trish. We gotta talk about the favor I mentioned. When you gonna be at the diner again?"

They decided Little Carmine didn't need to be at the meeting and talked over coffee after she finished her shift the next day. With the details settled, Trish grabbed her things and walked to the bus stop. She had a little shopping to do.

Her first stop was at the bank to cash in twenty-two hundred dollars' worth of travelers checks. She took a couple of deep breaths before going in. She hoped she didn't seem too nervous when the teller handed her twenty-two hundred dollar bills in an

envelope. She tucked it into her purse and walked out to catch the
next bus. Next stop was a hat store on Broad Street she'd passed a
million times but had never entered.

"I'm looking for a beret," she told the clerk.

"What size and color?"

"Geez, I don't know the size." She tried to remember how big
Vincent's head was. "What size would you wear?"

"Me? I'd probably take a small."

"Let me see a medium in black."

Trish tried it on. It was loose on her, but she imagined Vincent's head would take up the slack. She paid him and went in
search of the next prop.

Hahne's Department Store was half a block down Broad
Street. She located the men's department and an elderly gentleman waited on her.

"I'm not sure what you call those scarves men wear instead
of ties. Do you have those?"

"You mean an ascot, miss. Step this way."

She followed him to a shelf that contained ascots in every
color imaginable. Vincent wore only black suits, so she could
have chosen anything. After unfolding and examining four or five
ascots, Trish selected a deep red one with tiny gold stars for Vincent, and a solid green one for Carmine. They looked like what
she imagined a Hollywood director and assistant would wear.

One more stop at Kresge's Five & Ten for the darkest sunglasses she could find for director Vincent, and her shopping was
done.

Trish got so caught up shopping for props that she forgot
about the twenty-two hundred dollars in her purse. As she
remembered the money, she clasped the purse to her chest and
wound the strap around her arms, so nobody could wrench it
away from her on the bus.

She arrived home in plenty of time to bury the money and
props in a dresser drawer beneath her pajamas, sure no thief
would look there. She felt foolish worrying about somebody
stealing twenty-two hundred dollars when they'd lived with a
bag containing ninety-six thousand dollars for months after Mr.
C's death.

Trish called Mary to finalize the only untethered part of her
plan. "I need you to cover for me. I have to go out of town to

arrange a surprise for Gabby, and I don't want her to know. I told her I need time away for a couple of days with you before we move. Will you go along with it? Please?"

"I...I don't know, Trish. Isn't there any other way? I hate to lie to Gabby."

"It's the only story she'll believe. I tried to think of something else, but I can't trust anyone the way I trust you. She won't find out. I promise."

"If you're sure."

Trish gave Mary the dates and said she'd touch base when she got back.

"HAVE A GOOD time and don't get sunburned. Give Mary a hug for me," Gabby said, as she walked Trish to the door carrying her suitcase. "You sure you've got enough money?"

"Umm." Trish took Gabby by the shoulders and kissed her on the forehead, her nose, and then lingered on her mouth, gently sliding her tongue in before pulling back. "I'd better go before I change my mind," she said. "I'll be back Saturday, babe. I love you." Trish turned to wave before closing the outside door.

Chapter Twenty-five

INSTEAD OF SLEEPING, Trish inventoried every crack in the ceiling of room sixteen at the Clover Leaf Motel. She also memorized the precise position and width of every chip in the plastic casing of the alarm clock on the nightstand. Given the task that faced them, she hoped Vincent and Little Carmine had spent a more restful night.

Vincent had visited Father D'Alessio the previous afternoon, so he was able to identify him boarding the bus to New Haven that morning, even wearing civilian clothes. "Okay, here we go," Vincent declared, as soon as the Greyhound bus eased out of the Gloversville station.

He wheeled the black Cadillac out of the parking lot and, minutes later, coasted to the curb in front of the church. While he and Little Carmine unloaded the U-Haul trailer, Trish unlocked the front door with the key Father D'Alessio had given Vincent. In addition to the ladder, they carried in a few large empty cartons for appearances and Trish taped a sign to the outside door and locked it.

Vincent checked all interior doors and Trish became alarmed when he disappeared into the church office.

"Why are you going in there?"

"Just checking to be sure nobody's here. Besides, I figure there's a bathroom in there."

In a few minutes, the sound of a flushing toilet echoed off the walls of the old stone church. Vincent returned, removed his sunglasses and beret, and tossed them onto the pew where Trish sat waiting. The men removed their suit jackets and slipped on coveralls. Little Carmine secured his with huge safety pins like the kind Trish had used to fasten diapers on the littlest kids.

"This is it." Trish pointed to the painting of San Salvador. "You gotta be real careful with it. I'm sure it's valuable."

Vincent positioned the ladder in front of the wall, climbed to the fifth step, and balanced carefully before reaching for the frame. He worked his fingers expertly around the top and felt behind it.

"It's got a wire. I'm gonna lift it off and hand it to you," he said to Little Carmine. "Trish, you might have to help him with it."

Trish stood next to Little Carmine and waited, all the while not breathing. She didn't know what she expected to see behind the painting, but she knew something had to be there. She spread a blanket on the pew and guided him in placing it out of harm's way. Once it was stable, she turned her attention to the wall.

In her dreams, the loose stone was clearly identifiable because it was a slightly different color from the others. She strained to see anything that looked different in the dull light. All she saw were the two nails that had held the wire.

Vincent placed his ear next to the wall and tapped on the stones with a screwdriver handle. He tried each stone. Then, he ran his fingers over the mortar between the stones before stopping to remove a penknife from his overalls pocket. Using the tip of the blade, he tested the mortar in a couple of places to see if it would give under slight pressure. Nothing loosened. His muttering did not inspire Trish's confidence.

Little Carmine and Vincent spoke rapidly in Italian and Vincent turned to Trish when he stepped off the ladder. Shaking his head, he said, "Ain't nothing in this wall."

"You sure?"

"Yeah, these walls are solid. C'mere. See for yourself." He pulled out a small flashlight and shined it along the mortar. "See? It's all the same color. If one of those stones was put in after the others, the mortar would look different. I was an apprentice to a stonemason. I know this stuff."

"Couldn't there be a hollow space behind the stones?"

Vincent climbed back on the ladder and tapped the stones. "Listen. If it was hollow, it would sound different. You try it." He got off the ladder and held out a hand for Trish. She climbed slowly and reached for the screwdriver Vincent extended.

Trish tapped and listened to the solid sound that proved her theory was wrong. She tapped harder, knowing she'd wasted twenty-two hundred dollars on what Gabby said was a wild goose chase. She felt a choking sensation and accepted Carmine's help getting off the ladder. She handed him the screwdriver and walked to the side door leading to the cemetery.

"Where you goin?" Little Carmine called. "You okay?"

"I need some air."

Trish walked to Mr. C's grave as a wave of anger gripped her intestines.

"You son of a bitch, rotten son of a bitch. Knowing you was no picnic, but this...this is such bullshit. I can't believe you'd do this to me. I never did anything but be your friend."

She tasted salt as tears of fury slid down her cheeks. The longer she looked at his tombstone, the greater her temptation to smash the violin with a rock. She stood with clenched fists and was unaware of anyone's presence until she heard Little Carmine's voice.

"Hey, Trish, ya gotta see this." He waddled toward her with what she could only describe as a demonic smile.

She tried to wipe away the evidence of her embarrassment, but she wasn't quick enough. He handed her a silk handkerchief.

"Come on back. There's something you'll want to see."

"Check this out," Vincent said. He flipped the painting and showed her a false backing he'd peeled away with his knife. Beneath it, tucked into one of the bottom corners of the frame, was a small leather pouch.

"Is this what you're looking for?" Carmine asked, with a smile that engulfed the bottom half of his face.

Trish lifted the pouch and fingered what felt like pebbles inside. "Yeah, it is." She vowed silently to return to Mr. C's grave to apologize.

"I guess we're done," Vincent said. "Let's get the hell out of here." He suddenly crossed himself. "We should reseal this backing. If somebody besides you knew this was here, they might get pissed." He quickly crossed himself again.

Little Carmine reached into his bag of tools and retrieved a bottle of glue. He watched Vincent apply glue to the knife blade and spread it evenly on the canvas. Using his gloved finger, he gently pressed the fabric down and held it for a minute.

Trish and Carmine handed the painting to Vincent. He felt around the back for the wire and centered the frame on the two nails. "Is it straight?"

"A little to your left," Trish coached. "A little more...that's it. You got it. You guys put the stuff back in the U-Haul. I wanna light a candle. Give me a couple of minutes."

Trish put a dollar in the metal box. She lit a candle and sent a silent message to Mr. C. She didn't know what was in the pouch, but whatever it was, it was his last gift to her. She hoped he would forgive her tirade in the cemetery. Turning from the bank of candles, she said, "Thank you, my friend."

The goombahs rearranged the empty equipment boxes and secured the folding ladder in the trailer. Trish removed the sign, opened the back door of the Caddy, and suddenly remembered she still had the key in her pocket. Recalling the instructions Father D'Alessio had given Vincent, she returned to the church, counted six pews from the back, and tucked the key inside the prayer book on the rack on the left side of the center aisle. She placed it spine-side down.

"Are we sure we have everything?" she asked, once they were in the car.

"I almost forgot my disguise," Vincent said, "but I've got it right here. He tugged on the beret and slipped the sunglasses on before starting the ignition. He admired himself in the mirror. "Looks pretty good on me, don't you think?"

"Where we goin now?" Little Carmine asked.

"You guys can go where you want. I need a nap...ooh, I almost forgot." She reached into her purse and handed an envelope with the remaining thousand dollars to Little Carmine.

Vincent plucked it out of his hand and tucked it inside his jacket pocket. "The guy at the motel says there's a good Italian restaurant right outside the town. Wanna eat there?"

"As long as I don't have to serve the food."

"Seeing how you're paying for the motel, dinner's on Little Carmine."

Vincent parked the car and Trish slid across the seat. She saw Little Carmine struggle to get out, so she waited for him to open the door.

"Have a nice nap. We'll pick you up at six, okay?"

TRISH LET HERSELF into the room and dropped her purse on the bed. She removed the leather pouch and moved away from the window. Seated on the closed toilet seat, she untied the brittle, double-knotted string that held the pouch closed. It crumbled in her hand. She pulled pieces of string out of the holes and stretched the open end of the pouch. With her hand poised, she hesitated the way she'd done as a kid before devouring a special dessert. She put her hand in, wrapped her fingers around the contents, and stared in amazement at what she pulled out. Except for oohing and aahing at someone's engagement ring from time to time, she'd never seen stones like these. She was pretty sure she knew what they were, and remembered her high school science teacher showing the students how to tell if a stone was a genuine diamond.

She put the stones back in the pouch except for one and picked up a water glass from the plastic tray on top of the dresser. Holding it up to the light, she lightly scratched the stone across the clear part of the glass. It left a definite line. Her tongue stuck to the roof of her mouth and her heart raced as she tested each of the twelve remaining stones, and counted thirteen straight lines etched into the water glass.

"Holy shit," she said softly. "These must be worth a fortune. Wait till Gabby sees them."

Trish had no idea that within fewer than twenty-four hours, she'd go from feeling like the luckiest person in the world to wanting to slit her wrists.

Chapter Twenty-six

WITHIN SECONDS, THE elation that enveloped Trish on the ride back from Gloversville crashed on the dinette table where she found an envelope from Gabby. No heart over the 'i', in Trish, not even her name, just the initials 'TM' in heavy black ink.

Trish tore open the envelope and read, "I talked to Mary. I'm gone, but I better never find out who the whore is, or I'll kill her. I trusted you. Big mistake. You're a liar and a cheat." It was unsigned.

Trish raced into the bedroom. Gabby's side of the closet was empty — shoes, everything — gone. Trish barely made it to the bed before the room spun completely out of control. She vaguely recalled reaching for the wastebasket.

"Please, please be home, Mary," she said as she dialed. "Thank God you're home!" Trish said when Mary answered. "What the hell happened to Gabby? She's left me."

"Are you all right?" Mary described her brief conversation with Gabby.

"She thinks I was with another woman!"

"Were you?"

"Of course not. I love Gabby. I would never cheat on her. I have to find her."

"I knew I should never have agreed to cover for you. Now, she doesn't trust me, either. She didn't believe me when I said I didn't know where you were. Where the hell were you?"

Mary swearing was enough of a shock to jolt Trish back from the edge of hysteria. "Please, don't you turn on me, too. I'll explain later, but right now I have to find Gabby. I'll call you back."

"Take deep breaths. Calm down," Trish said, repeatedly while opening the closet door. Could Gabby have gone back to Puerto Rico? She pulled the black bag out and discovered the zipper was jammed, leaving only a two-inch opening. "Shit." She remembered doing that before leaving for Gloversville. She slipped three fingers inside the narrow opening and tipped the bag upside down. The stacks of traveler's checks and money orders seemed intact.

She rushed to the kitchen and phoned the diner. "Ro, I'm back. Just wanted to let you know."

"Not a minute too soon. Listen, don't tell her I said this, but Gabby's been so bitchy I thought she was gonna get fired. Last night, one of her customers found a hair in her sandwich and I thought Gabby was gonna kill her. Lucky it was near the end of her shift. I took the woman a new sandwich and told Gabby to chill."

"Must be her time of the month. I'm on at eleven tomorrow. See you then."

Trish hoped when she showed Gabby what she brought back, she'd believe she wasn't cheating. Trish knew Vincent and Little Carmine would back her up, but who wanted to use them for character witnesses?

Trish called Mary back. "She was at work last night, but that's all I know. Why'd she call you anyway?"

"She called to talk to Otilio, and I happened to pick up the phone. She wanted him to help her shop for a car, a surprise for you. She said she needed a car to pack things for the move to Pennsylvania, and she was planning to teach you to drive. Looks like she got the biggest surprise."

"So, what'd you tell her?"

"I admitted that I knew you went away by yourself and that you told her I was with you, but that's all I knew. She as much as called me a liar. At first, she worried that something had happened to you, but quickly she concluded you must be off on a fling with another woman. She mumbled something about stuff she found in a drawer, a beret and sunglasses. She was so hysterical I couldn't understand half of what she said. You know how her accent gets when she's excited. I tried to calm her down, but she kept insisting there was no reason you'd lie to her unless you were with another woman."

TRISH SKIPPED BREAKFAST the next morning and settled for a cup of Sanka. She rinsed out the clothes she'd worn on the trip and ironed a uniform, but no matter what she did to fill the hours before it was time to go to work, her focus remained on

Gabby. Twice she reapplied her makeup only to have it run down her face in a torrent of tears.

She walked to the bus stop but, when she reached the corner, she couldn't remember how she got there. She tried to tell herself to snap out of it, but her brain seemed encased in concrete. Panic remained barely beneath the surface during the bus ride. Like a broken record, her internal voice repeated that Gabby would never come back, and that it was justified because she'd lied to her.

Like a robot, Trish dismounted the bus and put one foot in front of the other until she stood in front of Scotty's. For a few minutes, she looked through the windows to see if Gabby was there. She'd done the schedule and knew she should be, but she didn't see her. She went inside.

Rosalie came up to Trish as she hung her coat on a hook in the dressing area behind the kitchen. "I tried to call you, but you must have left. You need to get into the Ladies. Barbara's in there with Gabby. She's off the wall. The boss will be here soon, and I'm worried he'll fire her."

"Here, take this for me." Trish shoved her purse at Rosalie and walked to the other end of the diner as fast as she could. She heard Gabby's voice as she approached the bathroom door. "I'll take care of this," she said to Barbara. "Cover for me for a few, okay?"

Trish took Gabby by the shoulders and blurted out, "Babe, listen to me. I was not cheating on you. I love you more than my life. I went to Gloversville. I knew you didn't want me to go, so I didn't tell you."

Trish couldn't tell if Gabby's eyes burned with hatred or something else. Gabby shrugged Trish's hands off her shoulders. Trish stood for a few seconds before holding her arms out and hoped Gabby wouldn't attack her. Finally, Gabby stepped into her arms and grasped Trish so tightly she could hardly breathe."

"I want you to come home where you belong," Trish whispered into Gabby's curls. They held each other in silence until Trish stepped back. She wiped Gabby's mascara off her cheeks and asked, "Do you think you should say you're sick and leave?"

Gabby shook her head. "I don't want to be by myself."

"Then wash your face and let's get back to work. I'll tell the boss I have to leave early, and we'll both go home after your shift, okay? I'll tell you everything. I swear to God. Please tell me you'll come home."

Trish strained to hear Gabby reply softly, "Okay, but just to talk."

The girls pitched in to handle Gabby's station. One customer flagged Trish down.

"This isn't what I ordered." Trish took the plate with an apology and asked at the next booth if anyone had ordered a turkey club sandwich. They had, and she apologized again for the mix-up.

Rosalie found a Taylor ham sandwich with fries on the pick-up shelf in the kitchen and brought it to the first table. Relief spread among the girls when the boss called in saying his grandson was sick, and he had to pick him up at school.

Trish tried not to think about what lay ahead with Gabby. Gabby looked so awful, with pronounced bags under her bloodshot eyes, that the girls encouraged her to hole up in the Ladies. Trish fought the temptation to give two weeks' notice. She vowed that if Gabby forgave her, the lie that caused this mess would be the last that would ever leave her mouth.

Barbara ran over to Trish and Gabby as they were leaving and pressed a fistful of change into Gabby's hand, tips the girls picked up from her tables. "You guys take care. If you need anything, pick up the phone." She blew them a kiss.

Trish slipped her arm in Gabby's while they waited for their bus. "I didn't think I'd ever see you again," Gabby said.

"Fat chance. You're stuck with me." She forced a smile, but Gabby's face remained drawn.

GABBY ENTERED THE apartment tentatively and draped her coat over a dinette chair rather than hang it in the closet. Over cups of Sanka, they rehashed the preceding days. Apologizing didn't come easily to Trish and despite her sincerity, looking at Gabby's tear-stained face, she was unsure if Gabby would forgive her.

"Why did you think I ran off with another woman?"

"First of all, about a week ago I found a shopping bag in the pajama drawer with a beret and sunglasses. I remember you saying a few times you wish you could be more sophisticated like

New Yorkers, so after I talked to Mary, I went to look for the bag. When I found it gone, I assumed you ran off with someone sophisticated and were planning to dump me."

"Only you could concoct such a story. I thought we worked through all that jealousy crap years ago."

When Gabby looked down, tears dripped off her nose and chin.

"Let me show you what I found behind the painting in the church." Trish got up and started toward the bedroom.

Gabby raised her voice. "I don't care how much money you found. Money isn't gonna fix the hole you punched in my heart. I'll never be able to trust you again."

Trish felt electricity surge through her body. She turned to Gabby, clenched her fists, and squeezed until her nails dug into her palms. "It was perfectly okay for you to lie to me about your sick sister and put me through Hell worrying you wouldn't come back from San Juan, but you can't forgive me for lying about where I went? You want to know why I didn't tell you? Because ever since you quit drinking, I've been worried sick that you'd start again if you got too stressed out. I lied to spare you stress. And you have such little faith in me that as soon as you found out Mary wasn't with me, you didn't trust me enough to wait to find out what I had to say? You say you can't trust me? Sounds like you never trusted me to begin with, even though I haven't looked at another woman since I met you." Trish took a deep breath and expelled the air in a loud hiss. "Well, say something, Goddammit."

"I don't want to love you anymore," Gabby said softly.

Trish stopped breathing.

"But I can't help it," Gabby continued. "Without you, I have nothing. I was so excited about moving to the house in Stroudsburg and starting a new life. I already planned what to plant in the garden, and thought of names for our dog, and getting a car so I could teach you to drive."

"There's no reason we can't do those things. You have to decide if you can forgive me and come back home. I don't know if you're madder because I lied, or because you thought I was cheating. I've never given you a reason to be jealous, but I guess you and I are alike in a way. We have such a good thing together, maybe we wonder if we deserve it. We're good for each other, babe. Don't throw it away."

Gabby looked into Trish's eyes. "I have to know something. Are you willing to give the money you found away? I'm sure it was stolen, and it's not right to keep it."

"I've been trying to tell you. I didn't find money." She got up and left the room.

When she returned, she put the leather pouch on the table in front of Gabby. "This is what I found. Go ahead. Open it."

Gabby stared at the stones in her hand.

"They're diamonds. At first, I was shocked, too, but then I remembered something Mr. C told me and it all made sense. His parents worried about carrying cash when they left Sicily, so they sewed diamonds into the hem of his mother's coat. The stones were from the dowry his grandfather got from his wife's family. He didn't trust banks, so he bought diamonds. When Mr. C's father decided to move the family, his father insisted he take some of the stones to America."

"So Mr. C's father hid them in the church?"

"I guess so. I bet they sold some of them and gave him the cash when he left Gloversville. It's probably where the money in the black bag came from."

"What about the newspaper story we found?"

"The only one who could answer that was Mr. C. Maybe he did knock somebody up and that's why he had to leave Gloversville. I don't think we'll ever know."

"I was sure the money was stolen, and I thought you agreed. I didn't want our lives to depend on stolen money."

"Me either, but it looks like Mr. C wasn't a bank robber."

"Gabby put the stones on the table. "What are you gonna do with these?"

"Depends. I thought we could decide together."

For a few seconds Trish glimpsed the old Gabby, but then the grave façade overtook her face.

"Look, I'm moving to Stroudsburg, and I'd like you to come with me if you still want to be with me. If you don't, I'll understand. Either way, I'll give you half the money and half the diamonds. You can take your share and go back to Puerto Rico, or do whatever you want."

Trish had never noticed how loud the ticking of the wall clock was. She chewed the inside of her cheek and sat for what seemed like an eternity. She felt the happiness she'd known with Gabby slipping away as she waited.

Finally, Gabby looked directly at Trish. "Who gets six?"

Trish jumped up from her seat and began to walk away when she heard Gabby's chair scrape on the floor and felt a hand tugging on her arm.

"I'm going to get my things. Will you help me?"

"But I thought..."

"If you still love me, even though I get crazy sometimes, I want to come home."

GABBY RETRIEVED HER things from a friend's apartment and for the next few weeks she and Trish tried to put the recent struggles behind them. They kept their jobs at the diner until it was time to give notice and break their lease. Packing together for the move to Pennsylvania turned out to be a healing exercise, as they uncovered items that reminded them of good times with each other and friends.

One night, after what turned out to be their final takeout dinner from the Chop Stick Inn, Trish pushed aside the cartons and dishes and looked at Gabby.

"There's one more thing I need to tell you, babe."

Gabby leaned back in her chair. "Is it another lie?"

"No, I swear. I think you'll like what I found out about Ignazzio."

"Jesus, Maria y Jose, is he still around? I thought we lost him."

"Well, we did, but now I know who hired him and why. It never made sense that he knew so much about Mr. C and showed up in our lives right after he died. All we knew was what we learned when we found his ID from the Pinkerton Agency. Even after finding the diamonds and remembering where Mr. C got them from, it still didn't answer the question about Ignazzio. I wasn't ready to let that go, so I got some help from Vincent."

"The goombah?

"Yeah. For another thousand bucks, he agreed to check out Ignazzio and find out who hired him. I figured it was worth peace of mind, and boy, am I glad I did it."

"Are we gonna have to give the diamonds back?"

"No, they're ours to keep. Luck is definitely on our side."

Over the next half hour, Trish summarized what Vincent's investigation uncovered.

"You remember what I told you about Mr. C's family sewing the diamonds in the hem of his mother's coat when they came over here on the boat from Sicily?"

"Right. You said his grandfather used his wife's dowry to buy the diamonds cause he didn't trust banks."

"Yeah. It turns out his grandmother's family used money for her dowry that didn't exactly belong to them. Her father was in the Mafia, and he stole from some other Mafia guys to come up with a dowry for his daughter."

"Jesus, what kind of family did Mr. C come from?"

"Colorful, to say the least."

"This sounds like a movie."

"Anyway, to make a long story short, the families who got ripped off eventually found out about it. By the time they realized it, the perp was dead, so they spent years trying to find out what happened to their money. They managed to track down Mr. C's family in Gloversville. That must be when Mr. C's father hid the diamonds in the church and sold some to give Mr. C money to go to New Jersey."

"So that's where Mr. C's money came from?"

"Yep, and that's another reason why he changed his name."

"You telling me that the Mafia guys in Sicily hired Ignazzio?"

"That's what Vincent learned. He says he used connections he still had in Sicily but didn't say what they were. All I know is, and here's the best part, that big earthquake that hit Sicily a few months ago? It hit in exactly the right spot. It wiped out the family that hired Ignazzio—all of them. In fact, Irwin Greenberg, the phony Ignazzio, never got paid and Pinkerton's had to write off his expenses as a loss."

Gabby sat open-mouthed trying to digest all that Trish had told her. Finally, she spoke. "So, nobody's looking for the diamonds?"

"That's right. With a little help from Mother Nature in Sicily, there's nobody left who would know anything about the stones."

"What about Vincent? He knows."

"No, he doesn't. He knows I inherited something in that pouch from a good friend, but I never told him what was in it. He only knows that the stolen money ended up in America. There's nobody left alive who would know about the diamonds except us. Once we sell them, that's the end of the story."

"So, Mr. C didn't rob a bank, after all. See? I thought he was too nice to do that."

Trish replied, "Well, I'm relieved to know that everything we inherited was stolen from gangsters and not innocent people. Now, for sure, we have to use it to help people."

Gabby reached to the middle of the table for the small bag containing their fortune cookies. She handed one to Trish and cracked hers open. It read, "You will find important thing."

Trish read hers. "Old friends are like gold." She folded the little paper and pushed it into her pocket. She lifted her glass and nodded for Gabby to do the same. "To our old friend, Mr. C. I hope he's resting in peace."

Chapter Twenty-seven

Stroudsburg, Pennsylvania 1957

DURING THEIR FIRST few months in Stroudsburg, night-time conversations often sounded like this:

"What's wrong? Why are you up again?"

"You're gonna think I'm nuts, but it's too quiet here. Except for those owls that sound like escorts for the Grim Reaper, it's too damn quiet. And those belching bull frogs need Pepto Bismol."

"You'll get used to it."

"Well, it's a lot to get used to. Remember, I never lived in a house, let alone a house in the country. Go back to sleep. I'm fine."

GABBY JOINED A garden club and enjoys being viewed as an exotic addition to the group. Except for the wife of the man who runs a gas station, none of the women have ever met a Puerto Rican. She appreciated the club president's attempt to make her feel comfortable by extending a greeting in Spanish. Though it sounded like "Bean Vendo" to Gabby, she guessed it was an approximation of "Bienvenido." She's got a green thumb and some of her blooms were selected for the plant sale at the local high school. When they have potlucks, Gabby always brings a Puerto Rican dish, and the women fuss over who gets to keep the leftovers.

TRISH, NOT WANTING to keep any more secrets from Mary and Otilio, finally filled them in on their fortune, including the story about the pouch of diamonds. At first, they were reluctant to accept money from Trish and Gabby, but Mary worked on Otilio and finally convinced him to accept help toward a down payment on a cute, three-bedroom house not far from where he works in northern New Jersey. Once Mary has the baby and

returns to teaching, with two salaries, they'll manage the mort-
gage payments.

During a recent conversation, Gabby said, "With parents like
Mary and Otilio, their kids are gonna be smart. No way do I want
to see them have to work in a diner, or at some other job that pays
nothing. We need to put money aside for their college."

"Of course we'll do it, but it's a little early. Let's wait till the
first baby is born before we talk to them about it."

Gabby counted on her fingers. "That's happening in four
months."

Otilio got a promotion to assistant editor at his newspaper
and insisted on returning half the money they gave them for the
car. Man pride, Mary called it, so they didn't argue. The money
will likely change hands again when the baby is born. Future
Aunt Trish plans to spend two weeks with Mary after the birth
since Otilio's mother works and all agree Mrs. Mulkern has
exhausted what little maternal instinct she might have had.

TRISH AND GABBY arrange with a local bank to sponsor
two little girls anonymously. Each month they deposit money
into the parents' account for clothes and other necessities. At
Christmas, the parents provide a wish list to the bank and Gabby
goes toy shopping. She wraps the gifts and delivers them to the
bank. Trish wants to set up a college fund if the girls do well in
school, and they're thinking of doing the same for several other
kids in town.

Gabby regularly sends money to her family, and last spring
she sent them plane tickets. Trish conveniently visited Mary and
Otilio during their visit. Some things haven't changed.

As far as the girls from Scotty's know, Trish and Gabby stuck
with the lie about Trish inheriting a house from her Uncle Paddy.
Trish often thinks about calling Rosalie to see how she's doing,
but she hasn't gotten up the nerve to tell her the truth. Since she
and Gabby have sworn off all lies, she can't talk to Rosalie without coming clean, so for now, she's taken the chicken's way out.

The biggest change in their lives is that Trish is now a college
student. She met somebody in town who urged her to take a class
at the local teacher's college. At first, Trish laughed it off because
she thought she wasn't smart enough, but the woman kept bug-

ging her. Finally, she went to talk to an admissions counselor. She's studying Italian. Too bad she didn't do it when she had so many people to practice with in Newark. In Stroudsburg, the only one she knows who speaks Italian is the butcher. She can now ask for steak, veal cutlets, chicken, and hamburger meat in Italian. He's added a few spicy vocabulary words she hasn't learned in class. "You never know when you might need them," he says.

A framed photo of Trish and Gabby in front of the Liberty Bell in Philadelphia adorns the living room wall, along with several photos of area waterfalls and sunsets over the mountains from their various trips. Gabby has become an adept photographer and recently had a couple of her pictures displayed in the local library.

She threatens to learn to ski next winter, and Trish knows she'll have to go with her to be sure somebody can drive home.

Speaking of driving, after a couple of harrowing lessons from Gabby, they agreed Trish should go to a driving school or they'd probably have had to break up. It took her a bit longer than she expected, but Trish finally got a license.

Instead of a Cadillac, Gabby drives a fire-engine red Pontiac convertible. Trish prefers a solid roof over her head so, as she told Mary, she drives an old lady four-door Ford. There's so little traffic in town, one would really have to work hard to arrange an accident, but when they go to cities, Gabby drives and Trish tries not to jam her foot through the floorboard when she goes too fast. It's better than grabbing the wheel, which Trish will never do again after suffering a severe tongue-lashing.

They've met another lesbian couple and several gay guys who don't live far from them. It's a relief to be able to be themselves with them, but otherwise, they refer to themselves as roommates. Trish is sure the people at the bank have figured things out. They know they're not sharing a house for financial reasons.

Gabby is still a little paranoid about their wealth, so they opened additional accounts in banks in nearby towns. Trish handled the selling of the diamonds and got more for them than they expected. It took a while to cash in all of the travelers checks and money orders, but the only thing in the black bag these days are their sneakers.

The nicest thing about having so much money is that they are able to fulfill their wish to help others. They donate to every charity around, and Trish swears she's gained ten pounds from the cartons of Girl Scout cookies they buy each year. They overdid it last year and still have a half of a case of thin mints in the basement. Everyone who visits them knows what they'll be served with their coffee.

Once a week, Gabby and Trish have either lunch or supper at the local diner. It's their little ritual and they watch the elderly waitresses and say, "Thank God we don't have to do that anymore."

The waitresses love them because it's not unusual for the tip to equal the amount of the check.

People in Stroudsburg may not have much, but they're good to each other. Two of the churches run soup kitchens on Saturdays. Trish and Gabby take turns helping out. They enjoy serving people, naturally, and they even cook sometimes. It's always a challenge for the ministers to come up with money for food, but they know they can come to Trish and Gabby if donations from the church members or merchants fall short.

"You notice we don't fight anymore?" Gabby asked, shortly after they moved.

"Our house is paid for, you can send whatever you want to your family, and we can help out others. What's to fight about?"

WHEN THE WEATHER is nice, they have picnics in the state park not far from town. They take their two dogs, a couple of folding chairs, and a cooler with enough food for at least two meals to placate Gabby who worries about getting lost and starving. They hike, and swim, and enjoy being out in the clean air.

They almost always go in Gabby's convertible so she can work on her tan. Trish covers herself from head to foot and laughs as she watches Gabby swing the big-finned car around mountain curves, her curls flying and the radio blasting polka music. No Tito Puente around the Poconos, so she's got a new favorite radio station when they're on the road.

At home, Trish has no excuse that Gabby's music will disturb the neighbors, so when Gabby cranks up the volume on the hi-fi and dances until she's ready to drop, Trish wears earmuffs. When she can't stand it anymore, she takes the dogs for a long walk.

Once in a while, Trish says, "I feel a little homesick. We need to take a drive to Newark."

Gabby knows Trish will be cured when they cruise through their old neighborhood, passing the graffiti-covered walls and the runny-nosed kids playing stickball in the street.

"Okay, I've had enough," she'll say. "I've had my fill. I know we don't belong here anymore. It's sad to see what's happened, but I'm glad we don't have to live here."

Gabby suspects the real reason Trish wants to pass by the dilapidated tenement they used to call home is so she can wave and say, "Thanks, Mr. C, for everything."

About the Author

Lissa Brown is the author of an award-winning humorous memoir, *Real Country: From the Fast Track to Appalachia* as Leslie Brunetsky, a young adult novel, *Family Secrets: Three Generations*, a semi-finalist in Amazon's Emerging Novel Competition, and two novels about the struggles and triumph of a gay boy to overcome bullying in the rural South, *Another F-Word* and *Family of Choice.*

She turned to writing full time after careers in education, public relations and marketing. Her essays and articles appear in several publications. An infrequent bluegrass banjo player, she lives with her spouse in North Carolina's Blue Ridge Mountains where she enjoys being in touch with her inner Heidi. www.lissabrownwrites.com

MORE REGAL CREST PUBLICATIONS

Anna Furtado	Tremble and Burn	978-1-61929-354-0
Melissa Good	Eye of the Storm	1-932300-13-9
Melissa Good	Hurricane Watch	978-1-935053-00-2
Melissa Good	Moving Target	978-1-61929-150-8
Melissa Good	Red Sky At Morning	978-1-932300-80-2
Melissa Good	Storm Surge: Book One	978-1-935053-28-6
Melissa Good	Storm Surge: Book Two	978-1-935053-39-2
Melissa Good	Stormy Waters	978-1-61929-082-2
Melissa Good	Thicker Than Water	1-932300-24-4
Melissa Good	Terrors of the High Seas	1-932300-45-7
Melissa Good	Tropical Storm	978-1-932300-60-4
Melissa Good	Tropical Convergence	978-1-935053-18-7
Melissa Good	Winds of Change Book One	978-1-61929-194-2
Melissa Good	Winds of Change Book Two	978-1-61929-232-1
Melissa Good	Southern Stars	978-1-61929-348-9
K. E. Lane	And, Playing the Role of Herself	978-1-932300-72-7
Kate McLachlan	Christmas Crush	978-1-61929-195-9
Kate McLachlan	Hearts, Dead and Alive	978-1-61929-017-4
Kate McLachlan	Murder and the Hurdy Gurdy Girl	978-1-61929-125-6
Kate McLachlan	Rescue At Inspiration Point	978-1-61929-005-1
Kate McLachlan	Return Of An Impetuous Pilot	978-1-61929-152-2
Kate McLachlan	Rip Van Dyke	978-1-935053-29-3
Kate McLachlan	Ten Little Lesbians	978-1-61929-236-9
Kate McLachlan	Alias Mrs. Jones	978-1-61929-282-6
Lynne Norris	One Promise	978-1-932300-92-5
Lynne Norris	Sanctuary	978-1-61929-248-2
Lynne Norris	The Light of Day	978-1-61929-338-0
Schramm and Dunne	Love Is In the Air	978-1-61929-362-8
Rae Theodore	Leaving Normal: Adventures in Gender	
		978-1-61929-320-5
Rae Theodore	My Mother Says Drums Are for Boys: True	
	Stories for Gender Rebels	978-1-61929-378-6
Barbara Valletto	Pulse Points	978-1-61929-254-3
Barbara Valletto	Everlong	978-1-61929-266-6
Barbara Valletto	Limbo	978-1-61929-358-8
Barbara Valletto	Diver Blues	978-1-61929-384-7
Lisa Young	Out and Proud	978-1-61929-392-2

Be sure to check out our other imprints,
Blue Beacon Books, Mystic Books, Quest Books,
Troubadour Books, Yellow Rose Books,
and Young Adult Books.